PRAISE FOR SAVING NEVADA

An inspiring and heartwarming story!

"Saving Nevada is a captivating story of one woman's determination to rescue and train a wild mustang. It is a story of perseverance, unwavering faith, and of the powerful bond between a woman and the horse who captures her heart. I had no doubt I would like the book, but I wasn't prepared for how much its message of learning to trust our own process and pace as we navigate the ups and downs of life would affect me. Saving Nevada is a beautiful story that will stay with you long after you turn the last page—and one I highly recommend!" –**Jennifer Marshall Bleakley, author of Joey, Project Solomon, Pawverbs devotional series, and Finding Grace**

This book is a novel but is based on a true story. Names, characters, and incidents have been changed at times out of respect for privacy, as well as some characters have been blended. Certain liberties have been taken to accommodate the story being told in first person by the author.

Copyright © 2023 Lori Hayes Author. All Rights Reserved.

All rights reserved. In accordance with the U.S. Copyright Act of 1976, the scanning, uploading, and electronic sharing of any part of this book, without permission of the publisher, is unlawful and is the author's intellectual property. Any use of this book, other than for review purposes, requires prior written permission. Thank you for supporting the author's rights.

Photo credit for book cover: Jerri Moore Morgan
Book cover design: Hannah Linder Designs

Published in the United States by Seaquine Publishing

ISBN: 979-8-9871000-0-4

Lori Hayes

Saving Nevada

BOOKS BY LORI HAYES

HIGH TIDE
COFFEE BREAK
ISLAND SUMMER
COASTAL CHRISTMAS

SAVING NEVADA

ALSO WRITING AS
LISA MORGAN—KIDS' HORSE BOOKS

THE CHRISTMAS HORSE
TROUBLED HEARTS
MYSTERY HORSE
RUNNING WILD

THIS BOOK IS BASED ON A TRUE STORY

DEDICATION

"SAVING NEVADA" is dedicated to one of the most devoted horse women I know, Abigail Hale. She has a heart of gold, a spirit of joy, and a will made of steel. Keep training and riding always because you are amazing!

THE MISTAKE

I tried not to overthink but failed miserably.

The pounding rain and rapid click of the wipers created heightened tension that mirrored my anticipation about tomorrow. I glanced in the passenger side mirror. Old Red, our empty and rugged livestock trailer, followed obediently behind us. It swayed here and there as we navigated down the curvy mountain road, rattling a lot more than I liked.

Nothing would go wrong. Besides, there wasn't a thing I could do now. I shifted in my seat, ready to begin a new, challenging journey with a wild mustang, one that held potential to change my career and possibly my life. My own personal mission to save a wild horse, and my biggest reason for entering the mustang makeover, was why we were now battling the rain.

"Are you nervous?" Chris, my sexy, bearded husband, asked while keeping his focus trained on the winding road ahead.

Looking at him was far better than watching streams of rain snake their way across the passenger window.

"Absolutely." I swiped a long blond wave of hair out of my face and tucked it behind my ear. "Soon I'll be staring into the eyes of my darling mustang." My voice sounded muted between us with the pounding rain droning against the windows.

"It will be love at first sight. A true love story between a woman and a horse," Chris said with a lopsided grin. He knew me well.

"Think so?" In all truth, I was already half in love with the horse who lived in my imagination. I just wanted the story to have a happy ending.

"I know so. You always grow attached to all your rescue animals." He chuckled, reaching across the seat to rub his hand on my knee. "A glance around our farm proves my point. That's one of the many reasons I love you."

"Love you too." I smiled, but thoughts consumed my mind about the horse that would be *mine* for approximately a hundred days. We didn't have the money to bid on the mustang at the end of the contest in Kentucky unless I won the competition and the prize money. Invariably, training would be quite a bonding experience for us both and letting her go after the auction promised to evoke in me a big dose of emotional anguish. I couldn't imagine selling or giving away one of my beloved animals back home, and I treated them like the children I wasn't sure we'd have. My life with Chris, the animals and farm, the small handful of horses I trained for fun, and the work at the hospital kept me plenty busy.

I can handle the makeover too.

Thank goodness for my mom. She had boosted my self-confidence by saying, "Haley, you can accomplish anything you set your mind to, especially when it comes to horses. I remember watching you ride your first horse, Trigger, with no hands like the boy on the beach in *The Black Stallion*."

Well, not exactly like that. I had a saddle and just dropped my reins. We got a good laugh out of that memory of Trigger, an old Arabian horse I had nicknamed Wild Man. That experience launched my dream of riding a wild mustang bareback—no saddle, no bridle. How difficult could it be? All I had to do was gentle the horse enough to progress from wild to rideable before Kentucky. I pushed away my concerns about contending against top mustang trainers, ones who knew how to perform bells and whistles like sliding stops and spinning.

If I won the contest, not only would I win the prize money, but the rest of my family—my father and sister specifically—had to acknowledge they were wrong about me. Instead of using the college degree in nursing that my dad insisted I receive, I wanted to follow my passion and prove that I could create a fiscally solid career as a trainer. I was different from my mother. She'd trained horses for a living but had financial constraints. The contest offered me a way to demonstrate to potential clients, maybe even to myself, that I had what it took to train horses as a professional.

I saw my business, Haley Horsemanship, as my passion, my lifetime love, my future.

No pressure there.

"I hoped to make it through the mountains before dark," Chris said with disappointment. "That's not happening."

"No rush in this weather." The spray from the truck ahead of us made me wish we had bought new wipers. "I'm glad you're the one driving instead of me." I had no qualms about tucking away my independent nature for the treacherous trek across the rain-drenched Blue Ridge Mountains in February. At least it wasn't snow. The fog thickened with every mile we drove, starting at Swannanoa Gap. How Chris had the fortitude to continue driving in the mess amazed me.

As the evening darkened, I closed my eyes, in part to shut out the bad weather and in part to catch some welcomed sleep. My plan didn't last long. The curves of the mountain road caused me to lean against the passenger door to steady myself, but moments later I reopened my eyes to prevent nausea.

"It's dark out here," I said. "No traffic, no cars to follow." I had wanted better weather for the drive home with the mustang in tow.

"We'll be at the hotel before you know it."

Before long, Chris pulled into a parking lot in Nashville to eat dinner and to gas up. Stretching my legs helped relieve some fatigue and stress, especially when I talked him into entering a nearby shop right before closing time. I picked up several cowgirl hats to try on but kept coming back to the same cream colored one with a buckled beige band. The femininity of the hat impressed me, but it also seemed durable enough to handle my upcoming quest.

"Buy it," Chris encouraged.

With money always a topic of concern for my husband, a hardworking crop farmer who managed the fields day after day, I set it down. He picked it up, studied it closely, and handed the hat to the cashier.

"Chris?"

"It's perfect for you." He grinned and paid the woman behind the counter.

When we climbed back inside the truck, I held the hat close to my chest. We drove farther in the fog, the rain still coming down.

"There it is, up ahead." Chris slowed the truck and pulled into the parking lot. Heaven's Inn, what a glorious name. Their bright sign cut through the foggy night like a welcoming beacon.

We checked in with ease, but later that night sleep eluded me. Thoughts played in my mind of searching through the herd of horses to match my number to the one hanging around my mustang's neck, and the first glorious moment our eyes would meet. I wondered what color her coat was, her build, her personality? Like Chris mentioned earlier, I knew I'd love her immediately.

I must have fallen asleep at some point but when I awoke, the world outside remained cold and rainy. At least the fog had lifted. I zipped up my winter coat to fight off the morning chill and slipped on my gloves, relishing the warmth for the short drive. When we pulled into the muddy agricultural grounds, a feeling of material inadequacy struck me.

There we were, towing an extremely old 1987 cow trailer among safer, more durable aluminum stock trailers and fancier rigs that were a better fit for the job of hauling a mustang.

Chris must have read my mind. "Don't go there, Haley. We belong here just as much as they do."

I sighed, suffering from imposter syndrome.

"Haley, money doesn't make someone a better trainer. You've got this."

I planned to hold onto his words for the next hundred days.

With my new cowgirl hat placed on my head, a set of emotions greeted me. I was brave, adventurous, and had an authentic heart. I inhaled a deep breath and opened the truck door to meet my mustang.

My heart rate picked up, beating faster as we climbed the hill to the registration tent for the makeover. A woman at the table extended a warm welcome, asked for my name, and handed me a number to match the tag on my mustang. I pressed the tag into my palm, closing my fingers around it. Finally, I was about to come face-to-face with my beloved horse.

"Halter, please," a solid man standing off to the side requested in a confident tone.

My halter? I swallowed hard, words escaping me because I had made the decision not to pack one. I wanted to train without ropes or artificial attachments and instead use body language and round-penning methods prior to haltering. I envisioned entering the championship finals, riding without a bridle or saddle as we performed our incredible routine to uplifting synchronized music. We would earn sweeping applause for our bravery and skill.

"I thought I wouldn't use one," I said, my voice sounding hoarse. This man intimidated me. For having such grandiose dreams for my mustang, I felt like a child trying to please her father.

He shook his head. "Nope. Not allowed."

Nowhere in the rules and regulations had it stated they required a halter, unless I had overlooked that significant detail.

"Bring one to me before it's time to load your horse." He turned to the next person, who gladly handed over a rope halter to him. Dismissed, I turned toward Chris. I'd have to locate my new online mustang friends and hope they had packed an extra. Thanks to social media and texting, I knew what they looked like.

"Let's go find your mustang," Chris suggested, taking hold of my hand, urging me to leave the tent behind and reemerge into the rain.

I tried to slow my racing heartbeat by inhaling a deep breath and letting it whoosh out with force, but no use.

Chris and I sloshed through the mud in our barn boots toward the tent with metal fencing containing scurrying mustangs. A gust of cold wind swirled around us, and the rain beat down against our coats. *Breathe. Things will work out.*

Just before dodging around a light stream of rain waterfalling from the tent's edge, I paused to inhale the earthy smell of horses mixed with the intoxicating aroma of fresh hay and rain. Scuffling noises sounded along with a strained whinny.

Chris tugged on my hand. "You'll be fine."

He always knew when I needed a little push and a hint of encouragement. "Okay, I'm ready."

He gave my hand a squeeze, and we scooted under the tent for an immediate break from the rain to witness the overwhelming scene unfolding in front of us. The horses dashed around the pen, pushing into one another. One smaller, meeker horse stood off to the side.

Unsure of how to possibly find my horse in the chaos, I studied the numbered tags hanging from around their necks. *No. No. No.* Where was she?

The meek brown horse standing off to the side had mud caked on her legs and mane. She observed the activity around her.

"I want that one." I pointed to her. "Small, timid, sweet."

"What's your number again?"

I held it out with a shaking hand and squinted to take in the mustang's number from around her neck. "Really, how did I get so lucky? That's my mustang!"

He whistled. "I'd say you have the luck of the draw."

A deep voice echoed over the loudspeaker. "Can Haley Wilson please return to the tent? There has been a mistake. Please report to the tent immediately."

THE LION'S EYE

How had the staff members made a mistake with my mustang draw?

This couldn't be happening. I wanted the easy, small, gentle horse standing alone near the fence.

Chris glanced at me and shrugged. "Wonder what's wrong? Let's find out."

My feet remained planted in the dirt.

He took my hand. "Haley, let's go." He led me back through the rain to the tent where my two friends waited their turn in line. We recognized each other immediately.

"Haley!" Katie said, wrapping me in a quick hug while holding her halter. I engaged in the greetings first before asking if they had one to loan me. Katie's curly, short-brown, and bouncy hair fit her personality well. "From the pictures you sent me of your farm, I recognized your trailer parked out there."

Great. I hoped no one else noticed Old Red until it was time to load my horse. I shook off the negative feeling and hugged Lisa too. I admired her flowery scent and her silky blond hair pulled back in a ponytail. I might have blond hair but it had a mind of its own, especially when the humidity rose in the South. "It's so good to finally meet you both."

"You too." They spoke in unison.

I introduced Chris and they shook hands as I stepped in line behind Katie, deciding not to explain the possible change of my mustang draw. We briefly chatted about the slow drive to Tennessee in the rain, and as soon as we finished the introductory conversation, I asked, "By chance, do either of you have a halter I can borrow?" They stood, holding their halters in their hands, Katie swinging hers from her index finger, as if they had known to bring them. "They won't load my horse unless I have one."

"I didn't bring an extra." Katie grimaced. "What will you do?"

I shrugged, and my heart rate sped up.

"I have one," Lisa said. "You know me, Ms. Prepared."

Everyone laughed except me. I embraced her, instead. "Thank you!"

"Hold my place in line. We parked down the hill from here, so I'll be right back." Lisa scooted off in a hurry, her barn boots squeaking as she scooted around a tent post and into the rain.

The line moved forward. When it was Katie's turn, she stepped up to the table and spoke to the woman, handing over the halter at the man's request. When it was my turn, I swear he recognized me as the woman who didn't think to bring one. The possibility crossed my mind that they exchanged my gentle horse for another to prove a point.

No way. I tried to stop overthinking. Besides, the horse acted unusually quiet, possibly sick. I had to wonder about her fate, to wonder if they planned to return her to the holding pen.

He switched tag numbers with me without explanation. Perfect timing because Lisa returned in line next to me with the extra halter. I passed it along to the man, who nodded in approval, and then Lisa stepped up to the woman to obtain her tag number.

When finished, we strode through the mud and around the deeper puddles to the horse tent. What fun to search for our horses together.

"I hope I get a gray one, even if they are rare." Lisa glanced upward as if asking the man upstairs for a favor.

"Wow! Can't believe these are wild mustangs from the desert," Katie said, her voice pitched high in awe as we ducked underneath the tent. "I'm not sure about the government roundups, but I'm glad they're here."

"Me too." It made me sad to think there were over 50,000 wild horses in government holding facilities, but at least we were helping to find them homes. I tried not to imagine these horses being rounded up by helicopters from public ranges in several of our Western states. Freedom was important to me, and I hated wild animals losing theirs. Some people stated there wasn't enough food in the winter or water in the summer for the horses, but others believed the roundups were cruel and needed to stop. Whatever my belief on the subject, at least the mustang program offered a solution to decrease the overwhelming number of horses contained in the holding facilities. They might be awaiting an adoption that wasn't likely to happen.

While the thought bothered me, the scurry of horses running around in front of us intrigued me.

Within minutes, Katie thrust her number in the air. "There she is! The chestnut mare on the end, but hard to tell the actual color with the all the caked-on mud." She snapped a photo with her cell phone.

"She's beautiful." I turned my attention back to the docile horse that was mine for less than a few minutes.

"I found mine!" A wide grin spread across Lisa's face. "And you won't believe this. She's gray." I swear her face lit up like the sun peeking through this cloudy day. "Now we need to find yours, Haley. What's your number?"

I glanced down as if I hadn't memorized it already. "Tag 6642. She's from Triple B, Nevada."

We separated and each of us strolled in a separate direction to search for her. The horses scrambled in mass chaos. The more dominant mares positioned themselves in the center of the moving frenzy for protection from intruders—humans. Their instinct made it difficult to see their numbers.

Lisa waved her hands at me. "There! The big bay in the middle."

The word "big" tipped me off. Surrounded by trotting horses, a big-boned mare hovered in size above the rest. She shoved horses away to stay centered in the group and pinned her ears when one didn't move away fast enough.

Please, tell me it isn't true.

Chris double-checked the number I almost dropped from my hand. "She's right. That's your mustang, Haley."

Unshed tears clogged my throat. I wanted a small, passive mustang, not the dominant leader of the herd.

Chris pulled out his cell phone and began videoing the horse while I stood frozen in place. Katie bounded up next to me. "You drew the biggest, prettiest one here. Lucky you!"

Lucky me. I would have gladly traded with anyone willing. Anxiety held its ugly grip on me, and I stared at the horse, unable to speak. The original excitement I'd experienced this morning plummeted into a pool of fear.

The mare—I couldn't bring myself to call her mine yet—pinned her ears and bared her teeth at a horse's rump in front of her. She guided the herd back our way and stopped to study us. Our gazes met, and prickled chills traveled in slow painful motion down my body and formed like icicles in my toes.

She raised her head high, ears perked at me, and I looked straight into the eyes of a beast, a dangerous lion. Not a tiger … no, this horse ruled. The way she held herself, chest puffed out, energy bold, convinced me I was a substandard trainer in an overwhelming situation.

Her black tangled mane hung in knots on both sides of her neck, embedded with clumps of dirt, but despite my fear, I could see she was beautiful, wild. Thick mud covered her black and dirty white legs. An unreadable tattoo displayed prominently on the shaved portion of the left side of her neck. Her face, although stern looking and beautifully chiseled, held a dingy white star square in the middle of her forehead.

Our gazes remained locked for a few alarming seconds, maybe minutes, maybe hours. Arctic goosebumps froze me in place and I fought tears. How was I supposed to train her in one hundred days, or even a thousand days?

I battled the urge to return home without the horse.

The animal tossed her head with unmasked defiance, and I shrank in my coat. Never, in all my years of riding horses, had I ever encountered a steed like this.

That calculated look in her eyes … I didn't like what I saw.

She was straight off the Nevada range. A desert horse, not a domesticated pet.

Lisa rejoined us. "She's spirited, all right."

I nodded, words failing me. I could stop this right now, walk away, quit. Except I wasn't a quitter. My mom had always labeled me as stubborn, and usually I preferred the word "determined," but I had to admit, this dream of mine had entered the danger zone.

I fought off rising panic. I had promised myself, and Chris, that I wouldn't back down, and I had made a commitment to help this horse no matter what. The mustang hadn't asked for this situation. If I didn't step up to the plate and bring her home with me, she'd sadly return to the holding pen, and I'd fail in the eyes of my family. People held opinions about adopting mustangs because of their reputation as being difficult to train. I had no choice but to prove them wrong. My dream of quitting the dissatisfying nursing job would otherwise never happen. Quitting the makeover wasn't an option. The horse deserved better.

I could do this. I mean, others trained untouched mustangs in a hundred days. Why not me? It wasn't as though she had any bad habits caused by the mishandling of unskilled people who meant well but caused more harm than good. Besides, I had learned skills during a mustang clinic I had taken in Arizona. The trainer had shown us attendees how to work through the tedious process of earning the horse's trust each step of the way.

Chris stuck his phone into his pocket and sidled up to me. "She's a beaut. There will be plenty of bids on her at the auction. Everyone wants a big mustang any man can easily ride."

If I was successful enough to make it to the auction. I nodded but still hadn't spoken; my words clogged in my throat like a stopped-up pipe.

The loudspeaker sounded overhead. A man's voice announced for the first group to pull up their trailers and to prepare to back them to the chute at the mouth of the mustang tent. Thank goodness we were part of the second group. This was getting real.

I stood by and watched in silence. Despite continued commotion in the pen, the staff guided selected horses into the chute without issue, affixing a halter on each horse, and sending them into awaiting trailers. Lisa and Katie's horses loaded into their stock trailer with ease. No kicking, no mishaps. We had planned to follow each other most of the way back home, but it didn't make sense to keep their horses waiting for an undetermined amount of time until it was my turn.

I wished them safe travels and extended a hug to them both.

"Stay in touch, Haley. Let us know your progress," Katie said before climbing into her truck.

"You too." We hugged once more before she shut the door. I watched them drive away, a void filling me. Maybe it was the cold, wet day, but when I turned my attention to my mustang draw, my limbs grew numb. Her bared teeth almost took a chunk out of a smaller horse's rump before the horse scurried out of the way.

"I need to drive Old Red near the gate. It's time." Chris watched me as if to gauge if it were safe to leave me behind, not that he had much choice.

"Okay." *But hurry back*, I wanted to say. I was anything but *okay*.

"Haley, have faith in the process," he said, pausing to take in my feelings.

I nodded but my eyes filled with tears. He slowed down to give me a long hug, rubbing my back with his hand, his embrace making me feel supported and loved.

When he left my side, I turned toward the mustang with anxiety dancing through my body. The horse needed a name, but the trend was to wait until the trainer—meaning me, Haley

Wilson—removed the rope with a metal tag hanging from around the animal's neck. I chewed my lip, but the act did nothing to expend nervous energy, so I shifted my gaze to watch the loading process.

Chris parked our trailer near the tent, and two staff members, one of which was the stocky man who had requested the halter, walked toward Old Red. Thinking Chris might need help, I plodded toward them. They appeared to be having an intense discussion.

When I reached them, I overheard the stocky man say, "The divider needs to be removed." He diverted his attention to the latch Chris had repaired, and in a low tone said something to another staff member. He turned back and said to Chris, "We're concerned about the latch. How far do you have to travel?"

"To Scotland Neck, North Carolina. About five hundred ninety-seven miles." Chris remained calm, but I knew from the way he stood with rigidity in his back, his shoulders shrugged tight, that his composure was an act.

While the staff discussed the latch in further detail, Chris and I finagled the divider out of the trailer and set it inside the bed of the truck. The latch issue remained a sticking point.

Chris rejoined them but I stayed near the truck. The three of them fiddled with the clasp and talked between themselves. We had come so far and invested so much time and money; what a shame if they sent us away without a mustang. Then again, I had contemplated leaving the horse behind. Maybe this was fate, or divine intervention, protecting me.

Chris glanced up at me and nodded. All was good.

I worked my way back to the pen for a safe place to watch the loading process while Chris stayed with the trailer. Wanting to log my journey, I pulled out my cell phone to capture the moment on video. The staff separated the mare along with three other horses. She trotted around, running into them, and then kicked out at the metal-planked fencing.

The sharp echo vibrated inside my ears and ricocheted

through my body like a bullet bouncing off a steel wall. I gasped to catch my breath.

Unable to watch anymore, I shut off my phone and turned the other way. Until now, the other horses seemed easy to load, but when the moment arrived for tag number 6642, the easy luck changed for the handlers. Curiosity got me, though, and I turned back to watch.

A staff member held a flagged stick in his hand and shooed her into the chute. She trotted into the chute halfway, then spun on her haunches and tried to run back into the pen. A man stopped her by waving the flag at her. She slid to a halt, turned on her haunches again, and ran deeper into the narrow portion of the chute. With no way to turn around or run out, they tried to slip the halter on her. She kicked at the metal fence, the echo once again ringing through the air.

I stood still, barely able to breathe.

Two men hurried to slip on the halter and fasten it before she belted out another kick. The stocky man swished the flagged stick at her, causing her to thunder into Old Red, but she blasted a kick at the doorway of the trailer as she entered. They hurried to close the door behind her and latch it before she changed her mind.

One of the younger men shook his head, and his words would likely haunt me for the next hundred days. "Good luck. She's a real bruiser."

I was in over my head, and the bold mustang would, in fact, test my skillset and confidence to the fullest.

I couldn't fight off the intimidation building inside of me. When I climbed inside the truck and pulled the door shut, I started to cry. Here I was, taking a wild animal into my care, to our home. The horse's safety was in my hands, and my future was in hers.

MISHAPS WITH OLD RED

They say first impressions are everything.

The mustang had left an intimidating impression on me. If I wanted this opportunity to work out well for us both, I had to change my mindset in a positive way. My gut instinct screamed this mare would take extra time and patience.

Not long after Chris and I crossed the slippery, rainy border into North Carolina, a car pulled up beside us, the driver honking and waving. The rain continued to fall in droves, but as far as I knew, everything remained fine with our truck and trailer. Apparently, I was wrong.

"What's going on?" I asked Chris, imagining the latch on the trailer breaking open on the Interstate without us knowing. I didn't dare continue the ugly thought. My concern often showed up with gruesome scenarios.

"Don't know, but I'm pulling over." He clicked on the blinker and slowed to the narrow shoulder of the highway. Cars zipped past, too close for my liking.

"Be careful," I said as he opened the driver's side. I didn't want to step into the elements until Chris assessed the issue. Maybe we had a flat tire. I had changed plenty of trailer tires on Highway 40 before, and Chris held pride knowing I had the ability to do this on my own, but I was glad I didn't have to deal with whatever the issue was today. I preferred to expend my energy on coping with the huge undertaking of being responsible for a powerful, caged animal.

I jumped when Chris knocked on my window. "Haley, we have trouble."

Here it was. I prayed for mercy that the horse was safe and alive.

I pulled on my coat and tied the hood snug around my chin to ward off the driving rain. As soon as my feet landed on the concrete, I slipped. Chris reached out for me and I grabbed onto the door to steady myself.

"What's wrong?" I asked, fighting off panic.

He exhaled a long breath. "We lost our back right wheel."

"Lost?" As in the entire wheel, not just the tire.

He nodded. "Yep, it must have flown off on the highway somewhere." He pointed to the curvy interstate surrounded by soggy mountains.

Unbelievable.

I hurried to the back of the trailer to check on the horse. She pressed herself against the corner of Old Red where the wheel had flown off. All eleven hundred pounds of her! And she shook like a cold, wet dog. Not good. The last thing I wanted was for her to go into shock.

"Hang in there, girl. We'll figure this out."

She snorted at me in response.

An eighteen-wheeler flew by without so much as slowing down or moving over to allow us more room. The horse reared but slid on the slick mat inside the confined trailer. She snorted and landed on her side.

"Oh, my gosh!" I lunged forward as if I could somehow help the situation.

Chris pulled me back. "It's too dangerous. Let her figure it out."

"The latch." I forced myself to step back. When considering the safety of the latch, we hadn't counted on losing a wheel and the horse falling. I closed my eyes for a long moment. This couldn't be happening. God willing, the latch would hold, and the mustang wouldn't break free on Interstate 40, or hurt herself if she hadn't already.

"There's nothing we can do. Wait it out."

The horse must be scared. A strong sense of empathy for the animal took root and held, like a protective mom concerned about the physical and emotional safety of her child. She was in a new world, outside her comfort zone, and distrustful of everyone. Against her will, we forced her into a scary cave with wheels on a freeway as eighteen-wheelers flew by.

The mustang whinnied to the only friends she had known, the ones that were long gone, traveling in different directions to experience their own journeys. My guarded heart melted into a puddle of water. The poor girl. She scrambled to her feet, slipping once more but gaining enough traction to stand. A pick-up truck pulled in place behind us, thankfully leaving enough room to avoid startling the horse. The driver waited for a car to pass before stepping out and hurrying over to us.

"Y'all okay?" he asked in a thick Southern accent.

"We're fine, just lost a wheel," Chris explained. I stood frozen and silent in my little spot off to the side of the road.

"I have somethin' for ya." The man disappeared around the back of his truck, and then rounded back with our wheel. "I saw it fly off about a quarter of a mile or so back. Took a good bit to catch up with you."

"Thank you," I said with deep appreciation, resisting the urge to hug him. He was an angel wearing blue jeans.

"Sure thing. By the way, I'm Mike. I'll help ya try to put it back on," he said to Chris, extending his hand toward us.

"I'm Chris, and this is my wife, Haley." We each took a turn shaking his hand. The horse called out again, and Mike eyed her with concern.

"She's untrained," Chris explained, nodding toward the trailer. "As in wild."

I saw the whites of Mike's eyes, but he didn't question why

we were hauling a wild horse, in an old trailer, through the rain-drenched North Carolina mountains.

The men worked to jack up the trailer and attempted to put the wheel back on. I heard a lot of groans and sighs. Thoughts continued to haunt my mind about the latch.

The cold rain slashed my face. I stuck my hand into my coat pocket to retrieve a wad of napkins leftover from our fast-food stop yesterday at lunch. I wiped my face but a chill set in. I shivered in my coat. The mustang had only her natural coat, undoubtedly soaked.

The crisp mountain air smelled of the fallen, decaying leaves that covered the rocky slopes like a shiny blanket. The naked trees pressed close together as if trying to stay warm. Thank goodness the temperature remained above freezing, or our situation would be a winter nightmare.

"The lug nuts are stripped," Chris said with a fair amount of panic in his voice. He tossed the wrench onto the ground a bit too hard. The clang made the horse jump in place from her pseudo-safe corner of the trailer.

The man scratched the top of his knit hat as if thinking about how to remedy the situation. "There's a service station off the next exit."

Chris's shoulders relaxed a little until he tried his cell phone. "No service. How are we going to get there?"

"Without a wheel," Mike said in a flat tone.

I choked down a gasp.

"Think of it this way ..." Mike's breath billowed into the cold air. "You've driven a quarter mile already. What's another one?"

He didn't want me to answer that question. Besides, he wasn't talking to me.

"I'll follow you in my truck with my emergency lights flashing. Just go slow and steady."

Chris nodded. "That's the only choice we have." He motioned for me to climb back in the truck, and he skirted around the hood to climb into the driver's side. I didn't glance back at

Mike, my mind too busy contemplating the safety of the poor horse in the trailer. If anything happened to her, I'd never forgive myself for signing up for the contest.

We were all she had in this world.

Chris clicked on the blinker and waited until the highway was clear enough for us to pull out. Our emergency flashers blinked in tandem with Mike's behind us. At least there was enough daylight left to ease the burden as we crept along the interstate while cars whizzed past. One exit away seemed like driving cross country, the silent tension in the truck causing me to shift in my seat too many times, my gaze never leaving the side mirror of Old Red following.

Chris turned right off the exit as Mike had instructed. "Start looking for the service station on your side. I don't know the name."

I stared out the blurry passenger window at the drab businesses such as a small sandwich shop, a hamburger joint, and a vacant industrial building.

Things will work out fine; they always do.

"There it is!" I pointed at a shabby gas station with pumps out front. There was a small, attached convenience store with an older man in coveralls exiting. Two service bays held cars on each vehicle lift with more parked out front.

Chris pulled in, and Mike waved goodbye to us as he turned his truck around to head back to the highway.

We parked away from the congestion of the service station. "I'm going to jack up the trailer so she's safer," Chris said, climbing from the truck.

I hopped out to check on the horse, hiding deep in the front left corner of the trailer. "That's a much better place than leaning against the door with the missing wheel and sketchy latch." The horse didn't glance my way. I scooted closer to the trailer, whispering soothing words to calm her. I'd like to think my voice helped but wasn't so sure. While I distracted her, Chris jacked up the trailer for support.

"Be right back," he said, planting a kiss on my lips before he headed toward the dilapidated office.

"Take your time." After all, he was doing this for me. With a small handful of fast-food restaurants along the country road and one other gas station, I hoped Ralph's Service Station served their customers well. I didn't want to judge a business by its tattered office, but I couldn't help myself.

The mustang remained in place until a group of kids with raincoats rode through the parking lot on bicycles. She spooked and scurried around the trailer in circles since we had removed the divider at the agricultural grounds.

I dared to press closer to the trailer to comfort her. "It's okay, girl. I know you can't understand me, but we're going to keep you safe. That's a promise." One I planned to keep. "We're going to fix this wheel and be on our way." If anything, the words sounded good to my own ears.

The mustang returned to her comfort corner, her heavy breathing filling the space between us. The distant highway noise hummed its steady buzz into the late afternoon. Automotive clatter echoed across the parking lot. She no longer shook, thankfully, and I continued to chat away with lighthearted conversation.

"Big girl, I promised Chris I'd be able to let you go at the end of the contest. How am I supposed to handle that?" The horse glanced at me for a hint of a moment. "I agree. That's why I have a farm full of rescue animals. He doesn't believe I can do it. Don't tell him, but I don't think I can, either. But we don't have the extra money for me to bid on you."

She let out an ear-splitting whinny.

My heart went out to her. "How scary it must be not to know who I am, or where you are headed." I cherished the budding connection between the horse and me, even if only imagined. This must be how a mother experienced a similar bonding moment with her newborn baby. If I cared about her this much already, it didn't take much insight to realize how much pain I'd experience when someone else possibly won her at the auction.

The only argument Chris and I experienced since we met

involved my favorite horse, Junior, the one whom my mom had sold without warning after Paw Paw passed. He had left Junior to her legally. The short version of the story came down to I didn't have the money to buy him from my mom. My uncle stepped up to purchase Junior but eventually sold him.

When the buyer had lost interest in riding, and my saving's account reflected enough money to buy Junior, I jumped at the opportunity. Chris considered my decision an impulsive purchase and questioned if he still wanted to marry me. I guess I didn't blame him.

His viewpoint reflected that of a crop farmer, never knowing next year's financial situation, so he always prepared and saved for any future loss. In contrast, I used to spend most of my money on horses. Through the pivotal experience, he realized the importance of horses in my life, and I learned about communicating effectively and saving money. Thank goodness we worked through the make-or-break issue, and we held a healthy respect for each other's perspectives.

But I needed to tread with caution. I had to find a way to deepen my bond enough with the mare, so she trusted me, yet protect myself from being emotionally crushed at the end of the makeover. Was that even possible?

Chris remained inside the office for a long time, so long that I questioned if they had the replacement parts to help us on our way. When he returned to the truck with a young man, they chatted and then worked on the wheel. The mustang remained in her comfort corner but at least she no longer shivered. The procedure dragged out at least another hour, but to my relief, they fixed the issue.

When we climbed back into the truck, Chris said, "Apparently, the mustang stood near the back right section of the trailer for most of the ride, and the lug nuts couldn't sustain the weight."

"Glad the latch held." A shiver spiraled throughout my body. "If she leaned against the side long enough to wear out lug nuts, think about what would happen if she'd leaned against the door with the sketchy latch. It could have easily turned into a disaster."

He stared at me. "Haley, don't go there. We still have a long way home."

"You're right. I'll imagine us pulling into the driveway with the mustang safe and sound."

Once we were back on the road, dusk engulfed us and the downpour continued. My cell phone rang, startling me. Sure enough, two bars had popped up, and seeing my mother's name flash across the screen lent me a false sense of home. I placed Mom on speaker phone to include Chris in the conversation.

"Haley!" she exclaimed. "Are you both okay?"

How had she known about our trouble? Her intuition amazed me.

"We're fine." I decided to spare her the ugly details and reveal only the basics to minimize her panic. "We had a wheel issue, but it's fixed now." Mom knew all too well how trailering horses went, having seen some of the same nightmares with hauling as I had. I knew she worried about us, and my insides turned gooey warm. I loved having a supportive mother who loved horses as much as I did.

"I tried to call, but no one answered for hours. I figured you didn't have service in the mountains, but then you never picked up." She caught her breath and let out a big sigh. "I'm glad you answered finally."

"Sorry. I left my cell phone in the truck while we were at the service station." My mistake. I knew better. "We're fine, Mom. I promise." At least now.

"A large section of Highway 40 is closed, impassible due to a major mudslide." Mom mentioned the specific location, and once again chills ran through my body. "I'm glad y'all are okay," she said in a quick rush of words.

Chris and I shared a look. "We just drove through that area before the wheel incident."

She gasped. "What timing. What would you have done otherwise?"

I glanced Chris's way again, and he shrugged. My body involuntarily shuddered. "I don't want to think about it, Mom. Guess we would've found an alternate route." Talk about diverting a nightmare. Goosebumps rose on my arms.

"If there *is* an alternate route. Can you imagine trying to drive home with Interstate 40 closed for a month, or longer?" She paused and made a strange gurgling noise in the phone. "What about overnight with a wild horse in the back of your trailer and the temperature dropping?"

I grimaced. Chris ran his hand through his hair, and I knew he imagined the same terrifying scenario. She was right, housing any horse, much less a wild mustang, in cold mountain temperatures all night in a metal trailer brought horrifying images to my mind.

The conversation made me worry about Katie and Lisa. They had left before us, but I made a mental note to touch base with them once I finished talking with my mom.

"I hope there aren't more mudslides or incidences along the way," I said as calmly as possible. I had enough issues to deal with. My biggest request was for the horse to settle in our dry barn tonight, and for Chris and me to lie in our warm bed and find sleep. Was that too much to ask?

"Be careful," she said. I promised to keep my phone with me and we ended the call.

I settled against the door and shot my friends a text to check in with them, but they didn't answer. Maybe Lisa slept while Katie drove, or vice versa.

The drive remained slow going, the wipers swiping fast. I never realized how dark the windy highway was at night until now. With the hum of the tires, my eyelids drooped. I might have fallen asleep for an undetermined amount of time, but my mind knew the moment Chris turned into our driveway.

The living room light glowed onto the lawn. I'd bet my mother stayed awake with nervous energy, waiting for us to arrive home. Thank goodness we survived the trip.

I glanced at my phone to check on Katie and Lisa. Sure

enough, Lisa had left a text while I slept. They had arrived safe and sound.

"How do you want to do this?" Chris asked, pulling Old Red past the house and down the muddy road toward the training barn.

I had planned every detail in advance, even having a Plan A and B. Not that anything so far had worked out accordingly. "We have two choices. We can contain her in the stall overnight, so she's out of the rain, or keep her in the round pen with the stall door open to give her more room."

Chris turned toward me, his lack of expression reflecting his exhaustion. "What's your instinct telling you?"

He knew me well. I often prearranged the details, only to change my mind if my gut instinct guided me in another direction. That skill saved me a lot of heartache. "It scares me to lock her in the stall. I'm concerned she might hurt herself, or me when I try to let her out." The rain continued to beat down, but if I kept her in the round pen, the mustang had the option to decide. Something told me this mare demanded being in charge. "Knowing her personality, I'd say the round pen. At least she'll have a donkey, two horses, and Gus the cow nearby for company."

"Good point." Chris shifted the truck in reverse and backed up to the pen. The tires slid in the mud, but our trusty truck stayed true.

When he shifted the gear into park, I zipped up my coat, pulled my hat tight around my face, and hopped out. *Here we go.* Our first night home with the mustang. We could do this.

I would do this.

The driving rain chilled my face. I fiddled with the latch on the round pen, my hands wet and darn near freezing. I slid open the panel. The floodlight offered just enough visibility to highlight a lone figure hurrying toward me. Eleven o'clock, and Mom had stayed awake to greet us.

She joined me at the gate as Chris backed Old Red into the tight opening to fill the space. "Great driving," she commented.

"He's amazing at backing trailers," I said, giving her a tight hug. "It's so good to be home."

"I'm glad you made it safely. And I'm dying to see your mustang." Her voice sounded giddy with excitement.

She always supported me in my horse endeavors and remained my rock.

Chris joined us behind the trailer. "Ready?"

I tried to rein in my exuberance, so I didn't spook the horse. "Ready."

Entering the round pen by squeezing between the trailer and the panel, I fiddled with the latch on the trailer, grateful it survived the wheel fiasco and the duration of the mountainous trip. It released, and the metal door swung open wide. I hurried to escape the pen before the mustang bolted outside to embrace her new situation.

Instead, she remained planted against the familiar corner inside the trailer.

I spoke to her in my soft voice. "Come on, girl. You've got this." Not that she understood anything I said, but I kept my tone light and encouraging to build trust. "You're okay. Come out and see your new home." I meant her *temporary* home and knew Chris heard my slip as well. Trying to remain emotionally unattached for a hundred days seemed unachievable.

The horse raised her head, perked her ears, snorted in answer.

"How do we coax her out?" Chris asked. He was likely exhausted and wanted to head to bed, and I didn't blame him. This was my passion, not his.

"I'll try talking to her." I used the same soft voice I had used at the service station. Curiosity must have taken over because she ventured forward.

At the trailer's opening, she stretched her neck out, body quaking, ears perked forward with interest. She curled her lip upward into the crisp night to sniff the unfamiliar environment.

Pausing for a moment, she rocked forward twice, and then with a bounding leap, jumped out of the trailer. A splash of muddy water shot in all directions and sprayed my pant legs, but at least she had decided to leave the security of Old Red. I wanted to close the metal door in a hurry, to avoid her hopping back inside, but thought better of stepping into the enclosed pen. Neither of us were ready for such a brave endeavor.

Chris left my side. "I'm going to pull the trailer forward slowly. You'll have to slide the round pen panels in behind me."

"How are you going to do that without her running out?" Mom asked.

Good question, and I refused to put my mom's safety at risk by letting her help me.

"Guess I'll have to move fast." I counted on the hope that the mustang feared me. Although with this bold mare, I wasn't so sure. I had witnessed her bullying other horses out of her way.

Chris climbed into the truck and inched forward. The horse watched Old Red move, watched me as I hurried to push the panel in place from the outside of the pen. No matter how fast I moved, a gap between the trailer and gate opened, but all went better than I imagined. She stayed safe in the pen.

"You okay?" Mom asked, closing the gap between us and wrapping me in a hug.

I nodded despite the serious apprehension that swirled around in my mind, making me wonder if I had the knowledge to train this wild beast. Training horses wasn't the problem. It was training this dominant wild horse in just over three months that concerned me.

"Let's go," Mom said, following Chris to the barn where he parked Old Red. I glanced at the horse once more. She stood at the farthest point from me, shaking and wet. I headed to the barn behind the others, wanting to open the stall door that led to the round pen to offer her a dry place to stay warm, out of the rain tonight.

Flicking on the light, I created an inviting ambience. The task was easy enough to manage safely because the mare avoided me. She watched me from afar but didn't budge. Just as well. I'd had enough drama for one night.

Chris and my mom left me alone in the barn and retreated to

the house. I carried an armful of hay and placed it in the far corner of the stall to help keep her warm. I double-checked the water bucket out of habit, even though I had filled it yesterday.

Curiosity clawed at me, and I grew brave. Trusting that the horse would keep her distance from me, I stood inside the doorway to watch her. The faint light overhead created eerie shadows across the pen from the trees swaying in the cold breeze, but it didn't stop me from standing there alone in the dark night.

"Hey, girl. I know it's been a long ride but if you come inside, you will be more comfortable than standing in the rain." When she turned her head to tune me out, a sense of dismay overcame me.

I didn't know why I thought bonding with her would be easier once we arrived home.

My intuition told me the horse had no plans to enter the barn tonight. I left the stall to haul an armful of hay to the muddy pen, staying outside the perimeter. I hated to drop the bundle into a puddle but had no choice since the pen looked like soup. I tossed it with practiced ease over the fence, and it landed near the water bucket. She showed zero interest in anything I had to offer, including hay. Instead, she hovered near the fence, trembling.

"Poor girl. If you eat the hay, it will generate heat." Nothing. Not even a hint of interest in me. I wished she knew I wasn't going to hurt her, wished she'd come in from the rain. She had no family, no friends, and I was the only one who cared. I tried to coax her to eat with an outstretched handful of hay, but to no avail. I held out hope she'd head into the barn on her own, if she knew what a barn was. It was possible a stall resembled entrapment to her, like a small cave.

The overhead floodlight silhouetted her as she stood still, her gaze averted from me. Once again, a protective, motherly urge overcame me, and I held a new appreciation for all those years my mom had worried about me.

After a thirteen-hour trip, the weather and the wheel incident adding additional stress, combined with the cold rain, the frightened horse needed to eat hay and drink water, so she didn't get colic. It wasn't as if I could call the vet for help because the mare wouldn't allow anyone to enter the pen or to touch her. Normally, I'd put a sheet on her to help dry off, but that was off the list of possibilities too. I was the one who insisted on signing up for the contest, to bring her to our farm in unfortunate circumstances. It would be my fault if something happened to her.

CHARGING HALEY AND ELVIS

Nightmares haunted me most of the night. I barely slept, dreaming about waking up to a horrifying disaster with the mustang. The different scenarios alarmed me. An enormous responsibility weighed on my shoulders.

Trepidation, with a slight undertone of excitement, filled me as I entered the kitchen the next morning. My precious baby followed me, a sleek black and white Boston Terrier named Stubby who I'd had for a few years. I stood at the counter wearing a cozy sweatshirt, a pair of faded jeans, and fuzzy socks, while pouring a hot, steaming mug of coffee to warm me up on this chilly morning.

Chris stared out the living room window with a coffee mug in his hand. I loved the open plan of our older ranch-style farmhouse, as I had a view of the entire layout except for what remained behind closed doors. "Haley, you need to see this."

I swear my heart skipped a beat. Had something happened to my mustang?

"What's wrong?"

"Come look." The casual voice he used held a touch of humor.

I strolled to the window. He inched over to make room for me to peer out at the round pen. The rain had stopped, and the mustang stood still, staring at the ground with her ears pointed in interest. Thank goodness she had made it through the bad weather last night.

Elvis, a cantankerous feral turkey, who thought he was a duck like his feathered friend, strutted back and forth along the outside of the round pen. Territorial as usual, I suspected he didn't like a new horse staking claim to what he considered his land. The war between two strong wills.

He paraded to the edge of the fence and poked his head underneath. The horse snorted. Not that I heard her, but from her outstretched head, perked ears, and flared nostrils, it appeared obvious. Her body language didn't deter him. He scooted underneath the fence and into her pen.

"Oh, no! Elvis, get out of there." I held my breath for a moment, watching as the two of them worked out their differences.

Chris chuckled and sipped his coffee.

Elvis darted back and forth, making it clear that he planned to establish the round pen as his. The mustang pawed her front leg and stamped her hoof on the ground, locking her intense gaze on him.

"Better get out," I said again, not wanting to see him trampled. No sooner had I said the words than the mustang charged Elvis. Right before she mangled him, he shot underneath the metal railing. "Too close! He needs to stay out of there."

Chris turned toward me. "And what about you? How are you going to train this horse if you can't enter the round pen?"

Good question. "I can't. I'm going to establish dominance somehow, and then I won't have an issue." I tried not to think about how the mare chased the other horses with bared teeth. "I don't have time to waste."

I planned to enter the round pen with her today.

"Haley … I don't want to see this horse hurt you over some contest."

I glanced away.

"Haley?"

I swallowed hard to buy myself a few extra seconds to think. He expected a reply that had no answer.

"Be safe. That's all I'm asking."

Fair enough. I nodded, but saving this horse meant a lot to me. I didn't want to see her return to live forever in a holding corral. "I'll be careful. For now, my mom is here to help me."

His brow wrinkled with concern for me. "Okay, I trust your judgment." He gave me a sweet kiss, and then headed toward the kitchen to set down his coffee mug and to grab his coveralls and coat from the hook near the back door. He left to start his day farming the field across the road.

I watched as his truck bounced down the long rocky driveway, shouldered by rows of bare pecan trees. The wind blew snowflake tornadoes in the massive pastures, unusual for Down East, a rural area in eastern North Carolina known for friendly Southern communities, small historical towns, and picturesque landscapes of wetlands and swamps. I loved living here, found it peaceful. The air smelled fresh, and I could hear myself think.

After Chris's grandparents had passed, he was the youngest and the only married grandchild not settled into his own home, and we moved into his family's homestead. I loved his grandparents' old farmhouse, loved this land. Seventy acres of flat pastures welcomed us with open arms.

Too impatient to wait for my mom to awaken, and with Stubby at my side, I pulled on a thick coat, a knit hat, warm gloves, and then slipped my feet into insulated boots. As I opened the door, a gust of wind blew in, and the rare cold blast surprised me.

Stubby scooted around me and into the carport where Ringo stood up and stretched as if I disturbed his rest. A rescue pup, possibly a golden Carolina Dog, Ringo sported the cutest ears, one pointing up, the other flopping over at the tip. Likely an avid hunter, it surprised me that he hadn't killed any of our fowl yet.

They followed behind me, sniffing the air to figure out who the new visitor was on the farm. I picked my way around mud puddles pooled in the dormant grass. Another large gust of wind blew across the flat open pasture, swirling around the pen, but the mustang didn't seem to mind. The delicate snowflakes turned to a light drizzle and sprinkled my forehead, the only portion of exposed skin that remained. I pulled my knit hat lower and shrank deeper inside my coat.

Stubby, who loved to greet all my new animals, took off ahead of me toward the mustang with Ringo following.

"Stubby, come here," I called out, but he ignored me. He ran to the fence and barked.

The mare stomped the ground, snorted like a bull ready to attack, and then charged the fence. She stopped just short of crashing through it, and reared. Poor Stubby yipped and scurried across the farmyard back to me.

"Don't take it personally. She's not used to dogs." I bent down and patted him on the head. I needed to practice my own advice. The mustang wasn't used to humans, either.

Stubby peeked around my leg and barked from a safe distance. Ringo paid no attention to the horse and jogged off in the direction of the pond. Not one to allow Ringo to leave him behind, Stubby ran after him. They hurried to the pond's edge to catch smells like bloodhounds on a scent trail.

I didn't make it far before Elvis scurried from around one of the three silos with his duck friend. The snood hanging beneath the turkey's beak flopped back and forth as he hurried in my direction with his black and white feathers fanned out wide. He stretched out his neck and opened his beak. The ungrateful booger had the audacity to hiss at me.

I stomped my foot in warning, as the mare had done to Stubby. He diverted his movement instead of attacking me but continued to make a verbal ruckus. Stomping must be a universal language.

I hurried past him to dole out rations of feed to the horses in the main barn and to toss hay into their stalls. Then I turned toward the round pen. No sooner had I reached it than Mom's voice screeched behind me.

"Haley Wilson, don't you dare go near that wild animal without me." She picked her way through the soggy barnyard, wearing an old pair of my muck boots, and made it to me in record time. "Unless you have a death wish."

The words hung in the air.

"I didn't plan to venture too close but couldn't wait to see her in the daylight." I knew Chris and my mom kept my safety in mind, but I, fiercely independent, found it a bit annoying. "I just wanted to watch her," I said with an inexcusable defensive tone even though I knew her reasoning held validity. "I know how to train horses, Mom."

When she reached me, she needed to catch her breath. I could tell from the glare in her eyes she meant business. I did appreciate her opinion and told her so.

The mustang watched with interest as we approached. She pointed her ears at us, held her head high with her neck muscles strained from tension. The red rope halter remained snug on her face and needed replacing. Right now, that seemed an impossible task.

I whispered, "Good morning, beautiful."

She snorted at me. It wasn't a pleasant greeting but an acknowledgement, nonetheless. At least she had me on her radar, and of course she would; she was from the desert and likely the alpha mare of the herd. It was her instinct to take stock of her surroundings for dangerous intruders.

Realizing she considered me as the danger, I lowered my gaze to avoid direct eye contact. I continued toward the muddy round pen with my body angled away from hers, then relaxed my arms on the metal fence. I needed to act as if she were no big scary deal, despite reality.

My mom mirrored my behavior. She wasn't well educated with natural horsemanship, and I had intuitively used the technique since I was a child. At age fourteen, I had been introduced to it formally but didn't learn until later about liberty training, a method free of ropes and saddles to allow the horse freedom to bond with a human. I learned from watching online training videos before entering the mustang program and flew to Arizona to take a live workshop from a well-known mustang trainer. For me, natural horsemanship seemed similar to the communication wild horses used with each other in the wild.

I kept my gaze soft. I couldn't wait to remove tag number 6642 so I could name her. One step at a time, and I refused to let her intimidate me. When she glanced my way, I ignored her to draw her in, as well as to establish that I was her safe place. After a second glance I rewarded her by walking away.

"Let's continue with the farm chores to give her a break," I explained to my mom. It took self-control not to glance at the mare to allow her a little curiosity about me.

"Think you'll make the deadline of a hundred days?" Mom asked with a hint of intrigue in her voice.

I tilted my head. "It's a long road, but I think we can do it." Tiny progress, but then again, she'd barely interacted with humans before. I just needed to remain patient.

Throughout the day, I continued the approach and retreat method, remaining outside the pen. My mom stayed at my side except for when she returned to the house to rest. Horse training wasn't a fast sport but was worth my effort, at least I hoped so. I focused on my goal of increasing her odds to find a good home.

When my mom joined me again late afternoon, I swallowed hard and tried to force away my trepidation. "It's time, Mom. I'm going to enter the round pen."

"You're going to do what? Don't you think it's too soon?" I knew her concern came from a place of motherhood, of protecting me, her child, as opposed to using a horsemanship mindset.

"Probably," I said, but I refused to back down. "The deadline is short."

My mom flashed me a warning look.

"At least you're here with me," I reasoned. Not that I'd admit such a thought to her or to anyone else, but her presence helped to remove a small percentage of my apprehension. "I checked online, and most people have either entered the round pen or have already touched their horses."

"Don't compete against what other people are doing," she

cautioned. She was right, but my competitive bone nudged me, and time ticked away.

"I'll try not to compare myself." I picked up my training stick with a small white ball attached to the end. The stick offered an extension of my arm to keep the horse's distance for my safety. "I'm counting on her curiosity. I want her to sniff the ball, nose it, and eventually allow me to use it to touch her."

"I understand the logic, but be careful and respect her strength."

Well said, Mom. The power of the beast never eluded me.

I fingered the metal links of a chain hooked on the fence and wrapped around the gate as a back-up plan so she didn't escape. They jingled and fell free. *Don't rush.* It wasn't too late to change my mind, but nothing rewarded a quitter, and I was her only chance at a better life. I paused long enough to close my eyes.

Please keep me safe as well as the horse. I need some help.

Sucking in a thin breath of cold air to build up my nerve, I opened the gate and closed it several times to desensitize her before I dared to enter. The mare trained her attention on me but seemed unbothered, so I slipped through the opening to enter the dreaded lion's den.

Inhale. Breathe out. Don't look at her eyes and threaten her.

I stood in the mud puddle at the entrance without clicking the gate shut. My kneecaps twitched and my mind begged me to scoot out of the pen, but I remained in place. Nope, I wasn't a coward but a brave woman who had a passion to save this horse.

The mare continued to watch me. She lowered her head in acceptance of my presence and yawned. I gathered my wits, which I had left outside the gate, and stepped forward.

She raised her head high, ears pointing at me.

Breathe, relax, and don't let her intimidate me. I was not a predator and needed to translate that information to her through relaxing my body. I made a point not to corner her, and I continued to avoid direct eye contact.

Her neck muscles tightened visibly. She looked as though she wanted to spin around and run away or attack me. Afterall, mustangs were flight or fight animals.

Give her relief. Look farther away and talk to her. I spoke in the softest voice possible considering my own set of nervous energy. "You're okay, sweetheart. I don't want to hurt you."

Using my peripheral vision, I saw her lower her head a smidgen, and mistakenly I moved forward. She began to trot around, so I retreated backward to the gate, not as a reward but to remove pressure.

Build a relationship together. Take your time. Those were the words I learned at the mustang clinic in Arizona. They echoed in my mind, but the remaining ninety-nine days ticked away like an old clock.

Eventually, I stepped forward again, taking a couple of steps. I held out the stick with the ball.

She turned toward me, ears still perked, but then she flattened them.

Mistake.

The moment shifted into terrifying slow motion. Her mouth gaped open, showing off her large, scary teeth. Lowering her neck, she jutted her nose toward me in warning, snorting at me like a fire-breathing dragon. Then the moment sped up into dizzying speed as she sprang forward and charged at me like a massive lion about to pounce on its vulnerable prey, about to tear me into mangled pieces.

I gasped, backing up in a hurry. With the stick and tiny ball held out in front of me, I flagged at her as if that tiny prop would save me from the wild creature. Five terrifying feet away, before she mauled me to my death, she stopped, planted her feet, and jutted her nose at me with intention, and then trotted away to the far side of the pen.

In a whirl, my mom opened the gate enough for me to retreat, and I hurried out. I bent over, gasping for breath.

"You won the battle. She backed away first." My mom rubbed her hand across the back of my shoulders, and I absorbed the comfort of her touch even through my coat. I remained bent over, my hands pressing against my shaking knees, while I dragged in the thick air.

My pulse pounded.

My mind raced.

My thoughts scrambled with incomprehensible words.

I dragged in several cold breaths of cold air.

"You're okay." Mom's voice remained soothing, calm, gentle, and she talked to me in the same tone I used on the mare. Her approach worked, note taken.

"Mom," I managed, my voice wobbling in breathy defeat, my legs trembling in my boots. "I didn't win. She charged me."

My unsurmountable fear crippled me as I spoke.

"But she moved away first."

I shook my head. "She gave me a warning, demanding I leave her territory. She won." She made me move my feet backward first, and when I retreated, she turned and released her pressure as my reward. "She trained me, not the other way around."

My mom crossed her arms. "What's next?"

"I don't know." I continued to drag in breaths of air until my breathing slowed. I had serious doubts that I had the skill to train this horse. Why had I thought this was my calling? The man upstairs had it all wrong.

Based on my research from people's personal experiences, wild mustangs weren't usually bold and aggressive. For the first time training horses, I stood on uncharted ground.

"I have to address it, or she'll learn that attacking wins out."

We were at a stalemate. Despite my intense level of fear, I had to push through this, not only for me, but for her sake. She deserved to find a loving home. If I failed, she'd return to the holding facility.

ROUND AND ROUND THEY GO

More research confirmed I needed to stop the mustang's charging behavior.

Immediately.

My mother and I stood outside the round pen, our warm breath billowing into the cold morning air. The horse hadn't entered the stall last night, but at least she had eaten today. I accepted any amount of positivity as progress.

I leaned against the metal fence of the pen to watch her finish mouthing the last fragments of hay from the dirt. When she finished, the dogs caught her attention.

"Good morning, beautiful," I whispered. She turned away from watching the dogs to assess me. It wasn't a bonding moment between us, but at least she didn't pin her ears.

The research I had conducted helped me orchestrate a plan and raised my level of confidence a few jagged notches. "We're going to have fun today," I said in a more hopeful voice than assured. In all truth, entering the pen again gave me pause.

She snorted at me. I counted on the day she'd greet me with a nicker.

I had a nagging hunch this wild horse would teach me more than I bargained for. I'd signed up for the program with the desire to learn about training mustangs and helping her find a good home, but I suspected she might also teach me about patience, perseverance, and whom I, Haley Wilson, was as a person.

She studied me with interest, the big star on her forehead reminding me of a bright headlight. I assumed that underneath the caked mud, her coat revealed a gorgeous buckskin color. It took fortitude to resist the desire to brush off the dirt, to rub her all over, to love on her. I had to find a way to convince her I wanted to help, not harm her. I dismissed yesterday's lofty goal of touching her, and instead took an emotional step backward with my new goal focused on setting boundaries.

Be confident, Haley.

Glancing up at the overcast sky, I inhaled a long breath before I dared to enter the pen again. *Please, keep me safe so I can help this horse, and fill me with knowledge and bravery.*

A sense of calm overcame me, so I fiddled with the chain links on the gate. She likely wondered why the crazy human wanted to enter her territory again. Hadn't I learned the first time around? I needed to change her way of thinking, and mine, and educate her that when I entered the pen, the territory became shared space.

Grabbing my two long training whips from the ground, which I called liberty whips, I entered the muddy pen. They were flexible long sticks with a longer nylon rope at the ends and weren't meant to use on her, but instead to create an energetic air space between us that established boundaries. Also, the whips offered me a slight sense of security.

"Be careful," Mom warned, staying close to the gate.

"I will." Thank goodness she had agreed to visit Chris and me. I wasn't sure what I'd do without her.

The mare turned, squaring up to me in warning.

I flagged her to the opposite side by pulsating the whips. Time seemed to linger in an awkward moment, the mare and I staring at each other in dead silence. Only a bird crowed off in the distance. I wanted her to understand I had no plans to leave.

Now was the make-or-break moment. I needed to move her feet instead of her moving mine to establish dominance. I pulsated the whips between us to establish a basic form of communication and a safe space for me. Without something so simple, I had nothing.

She raised her head and snorted.

If I wanted to be the alpha mare in her eyes, her leader, I needed to remain calm and not step backward to depict submissiveness. The silent communication was inborn in horses to establish herd hierarchy.

Be brave. You can do this!

It didn't matter that my nerves twitched from the inside out, didn't matter that I wanted to scurry out of the pen. I had no choice but to conquer my fear. Facing the scary beast head on forced me to believe in myself.

As Chris had told me when I first met her, "Have faith in the process, Haley."

She shook her head and powered with dominance at me, not away from me with respect like I wanted, causing me to gasp. I needed to deal with this now, so I created bigger energy with my liberty whips by moving my arms faster and harder to move her away from me. I swung the other whip toward her haunches to push her forward. To my delight, she trotted in a circle with me at the center. Progress!

To my pleasant surprise, she followed my lead as I directed, so I eased the energy between us. It was too much freedom because she then decided to test me by turning inward to run me over. *Think fast!* With the pulsating liberty whips, I thwarted her attempt. She respected my body position as I turned in a circle toward her haunches, my motion driving her to change direction. Another point for me, not that I kept score.

Instead of trying to draw the mustang in to touch, as had been my heart's desire yesterday, I drove her away to create respect and interest. If I controlled her feet by guiding her shoulder and hip movement with the use of my two liberty whips, I'd develop finer communication between us and increase my safety when it became time to step closer. My goal became working together as a team, with me in charge, instead of playing the dangerous tit-for-tat game between us.

A sudden surge of confidence overcame me. It was here, in this round pen, training this mustang, that I felt the surprising freedom from pleasing people, mainly my family in general and coworkers. I wasn't a healthcare practitioner at heart but a horse trainer. Horses remained my passion, my love, my possible future. I held the ability to succeed at training this wild mustang. Perhaps my childhood wounds had been holding me back from taking important chances in my life. I had always been a pleaser, and this was something I wanted to learn how to get over.

My mother still leaned against the metal gate, wrapped in a thick coat, gloves, knit hat, and a scarf. I had pared down to only a vest and gloves for outerwear. Funny how the weather had escaped my conscious awareness, replaced by my concentration on the animal in front of me.

I relaxed my energy to allow her to rest to avoid any sweat buildup or chill. In normal training situations, if the horse became damp in cold weather, I used a fleece cooler to soak up the moisture—out of the question due to the inability to touch her yet. She stopped along the fence and turned to study me, our first optimistic connection. What a relief for at least me, and I looked forward to the day she trusted me enough to relax. She wrinkled her brows with concern but awaited my direction, curious and intrigued. I mentally patted myself on the back, relying on my own positive reinforcement to keep going. Step one, creating a boundary, accomplished.

"Way to go, Haley!" My mom continued to champion me. She never quit, never stopped.

"Thanks." I glowed from within. I had faced a huge hurdle of fear and connected with a real wild mustang. I could hardly wait to touch her at some point.

I flashed Mom a grin before I sloshed my way through the soupy mud back to the gate, keeping an eye on the mustang in case she decided to charge me from behind. My intuition said she wouldn't. My experience said never to let my guard down.

I shut the gate behind me when my phone dinged. "Mom, it's from Lisa." She knew all about my new friends.

"How's it going with her mustang?"

"Not sure. Let me see what she said." I glanced down to read the text.

Hey, Haley. How's it going with your mare?

Relieved she didn't ask me that question yesterday, I typed back with more confidence that the training held real possibility.

Had a scary event but a much better day today. How are you doing with yours?

She typed back right away.

Got my first touch this morning and was able to rub her neck.

My ego deflated. She experienced what I had desired more than anything yesterday, yet nowhere near achieved.

Great for you! I wasn't about to let self-pity diminish her special moment.

Got lucky with this mare. She's pretty easy. What was your scary issue?

I hesitated, determining how much I wanted to confess without devaluing myself as a trainer. We had all agreed this mare was difficult, so I decided honesty was best.

She charged me in the pen. It was ugly, but we worked it out this morning.

Oh, wow. Haley, you are so brave.

I didn't feel all that brave, and my mom's forever label of me being stubborn seemed more accurate right now. It dawned on me how these unwanted challenges with the mustang were already helping me grow as a trainer. I could only imagine what I might learn in the long run.

I sensed the mare's presence near me and turned around too fast. She jumped back from the gate and snorted. Her curiosity surprised me, and I had to wonder if she had planned to initiate the first touch from the safety of me being outside the pen. I wanted to kick myself for spooking her.

"She tried to sniff your hair," Mom said, laughing. "Maybe

the key is to ignore her."

"Maybe." That often worked. "Isn't that life? It seems the more you initiate something you want, the more you need to chase it." I raised my hand to include the bright blue sky. "But when you release it into the ether, the desire magically pops up when you least expect. Guess it's possible we're closer to the first touch than I thought."

"Wise words, my dear."

I held out my hand between the slats in the gate, but the mustang kept her feet firmly planted in the mud. "No way will she touch me now."

Mom sighed. "I'd love to see your first touch, but you're on your own tomorrow. I need to head back home early." My mom had moved away from the gate and now leaned against the fence. I should have provided a chair for her to sit on, not that she would take advantage of it. She was used to standing long hours at the arena and usually preferred not to sit for a better view.

"I don't know how I can do this without you here." I fought off a moment of panic. Tomorrow I'd have to enter the lion's den alone. My mind raced and created all different kinds of disastrous scenarios.

"Stop doing that overthinking thing. Today went great and she almost touched you."

I glanced up, surprised she had read my negative thoughts. "It went well because you are here." My confidence had increased over the last two days, but without my mom, it waned.

"I'm a phone call away."

If I was able to retrieve the phone from my pocket. I imagined lying on the ground, trampled, with Chris in the back field until dark. I dreaded her leaving. The horse' size and sheer strength I respected.

By the following day, the progress I had made with my mustang—and yes, I admitted she now belonged to me, at least for the duration of the makeover—had all but disappeared. I tweaked the old saying to "One step forward and twenty steps back."

The morning was a bit warmer today, the sky a bright Carolina blue without a cloud in sight. I thought the good weather posed as a positive sign that today would start off better, but the mare proved me wrong.

She squared up to me, rounded her neck like a stallion, and pinned her ears when I approached the gate. She had acted fine first off when I had fed her, so what happened?

It dawned on me she was food motivated. What animal wasn't?

I ran back to the main barn, Stubby following me without Ringo, who had left us to explore the water's edge. I opened a metal trash can and fished around for a small handful of alfalfa squares, then I dumped them into a bucket with water to help soften them. Sweet Stubby followed me across the barnyard, and I noticed the mare observed every step I made.

I turned my attention to Stubby as he jogged next to me. "Are you my helper today?" He always sensed my distress and knew I didn't want to be alone with the mustang. Come to think of it, maybe the horse detected my apprehensive mood as well since my mother had left, which explained her resistance toward me.

I returned to the round pen and leaned on the fence with the bucket at my feet. My plan was to take full advantage of the treat idea and use it as a training tool.

"Good morning, beautiful." Other than studying me with piqued interest, she didn't greet me with her usual snort. I accepted her positive interest as progress, even if it was only because I had a bucket of treats. She related the bucket to her morning feed.

I entered the pen, jiggling the pail as a reminder I came bearing food. I made a mental note to start feeding her with a bucket each day while inside the pen, so she didn't equate me with the woman who made her work. I set the bucket down and backed away, realizing the risk of her territory issues surrounding food.

My mom's lack of presence left an empty feeling inside of me. I wanted her here but needed to persevere regardless and train the mare alone. Chris was busy with spring planting, and he had stated upfront, before I decided to participate in the makeover, how busy he was this time of year. In all honesty, I needed to prove to myself I had what it took to become a successful horse trainer.

Work at the hospital remained slow right now and thank goodness they allowed me to hand over my hours to someone who needed them more than me. Financially, the lack of pay impacted us, but short term we were able to sustain the hit. I almost regretted having to work there tomorrow because I didn't want to leave my mustang.

Too bad we didn't have surplus money to bid on my mare at the auction, to ensure she had a good home. My depth of emotion toward her surprised me, considering how difficult I found her to train.

When she finished eating her snack, she backed away enough for me to retrieve the bucket and set it outside the ring. Stubby sat on his haunches, watching me as if he were my babysitter.

"I appreciate your company, but you can go find Ringo. You don't need to take care of me." He tilted his head and whined. "Really, I'm okay. Go on, Stubby."

He walked in a tight circle twice and questioned me with his eyes once more.

"Go on," I ordered, otherwise he'd sit here all day and have no dog fun. He ran off, glancing back, and when I pointed, he hurried to join Ringo.

I turned back to the mare. "It's just us now." The look in her eyes seemed kind enough, but I knew better than to trust her. It was a brief, pleasant moment, not a change in her demeanor.

I retrieved my two liberty whips leaning against the gate. The horse raised her head and trotted away from me with intensity, which I viewed as an improvement over charging me. Staying in tune with her helped me to appreciate the slightest hint of progress to keep myself motivated.

Three days in and I still had no first touch. The red rope halter remained too tight on her face and tag number 6642 hung with accusation around her neck, begging for me to remove it and name the horse.

If I had more time to train at her pace without missing crucial steps, I imagined the journey would be longer but easier. However, the ticking timer wasn't my friend. Instead, I had to choose which steps to address, and which steps to skim over without creating drastic setbacks and a dangerous situation for us both. The last thing I wanted was to pass along a training mess for someone else to clean up after the auction. Not only would the horse pay the price, but my reputation remained on the line.

My horse was the last one in the mustang group to yet receive their first touch. Knowing that reality bothered me, but I needed to stay on course and remember the whole point of participating in the makeover was to find a good home for the mare. I just needed to train her enough so someone else had the ability to handle her and ride safely. But I had to touch her well before I could sit on her.

Tomorrow, I planned to attempt our first touch.

THE FIRST TOUCH

I met tag number 6642 just a few long days ago and already she had boosted my knowledge about training horses. I hadn't fully anticipated the long days filled with microscopic progress but at least I was learning.

Who knew what this sunny but chilly day would bring, but I held high hopes that I'd achieve our first touch today. I pulled on my winter gear and headed outside, the dogs staying close to me. At least the weather app promised us temperatures warm enough to wear only a long-sleeved shirt later in the day. Due to living on a farm and working outside, I knew to wear a plethora of layers, ones I could remove as needed. Part of me yearned for warmer weather, but spring meant my deadline would arrive too fast.

A male and female cardinal caught my attention, chirping from a naked branch of a pecan tree as if to entertain me, their birdsong a welcomed pleasure. The Carolina blue sky offered a beautiful backdrop and promised a beautiful day.

My phone rang from the pocket of my coat. I dug it out, thrilled it was a video chat from my mother.

I stopped near the silo before answering, glancing around to make sure Elvis wasn't nearby. That turkey was downright aggressive. I deemed the area safe and tried to accept the call with my glove but ended up pulling off my right one. I yanked my scarf down underneath my chin. "Mom!"

"Looks like you're outside. I meant to call sooner."

"No worries. I wanted to get an early start." The cold breeze blew on my exposed fingers, making them cold already. Boy was it good to hear from her and to see her on video.

"Early start, huh? What did you have in mind today?" My mother sipped from her coffee mug, and I wished I had thought to bring a thermos of hot chocolate outside.

I drew in a long breath of cold air before I explained my concerns to her. "Mom, according to the online group, everyone has already touched their horses. I'm the only one who hasn't. Some trainers have brushed their horses, and one woman has even leaned across her horse's back."

"Don't let the competition rule your judgment."

She was right. Taking the extra time to build trust with my mare had to pay off at some point. "It bothers me that I'm so far behind, but fast isn't necessarily better."

"That's right. She's the opposite of easy."

If my mom thought she was difficult, then I knew it wasn't me or my training style. "Besides, the easier the horse is and the calmer and sweeter they are, the more bidders there will be. It's also more of a risk of losing your horse at the auction." Lisa didn't plan to keep her horse, so no worries there, but Katie did want to adopt hers. "I run the risk of more bidders too because my mare is stocky and solid. Most men will fit her well, and the other mustangs lean toward the smaller size. But Mom? It will be hard to let her go."

Mom paused for the briefest second, and I knew she'd heard what I meant.

"Does that mean you want to keep her?"

Oh, boy. Did I really want to admit the truth since I hadn't discussed my feelings with Chris yet? Honesty won. "I'm growing more attached to her than I thought. I told Chris I could handle letting her go at the auction, but I'm not so sure."

Mom sighed into the phone. "Oh, honey. I'm sure that'll be tough, but it's okay to feel how you do. You're working long hours with her, and you're bound to get attached. That's reasonable."

Having a horse mother who understood helped. A lot.

My emotions tugged at my heartstrings. "It won't be easy. My childhood dream was to train a wild mustang, and I have the opportunity now, but I'm surprised at how strong of a bond I'm feeling toward her."

"I can imagine. What will Chris say?"

I wanted to keep my mustang, to adopt *her*.

Slowly my fingers turned a pale shade of pink. Plus, I couldn't wait to visit my girl, who watched me from the pen. I wanted to wrap up the conversation as soon as possible but without being rude. "He would say we don't have a lot of money to bid on her at the auction. At least he's open to the idea of me bidding a small amount, but our savings aren't likely enough unless I win the contest. He'd also remind me of other expenses to consider such as feed, hay, veterinarian bills, and farrier."

As difficult as it was, I promised myself to try to erect an emotional wall between the horse and me to limit the inevitable crushing heartbreak I was sure to experience when it came time to part ways. The problem was I needed enough of a connection with the mare to create an animal that trusted their person, be it me or someone else later, and to create a horse that wanted to please. It baffled me how to accomplish such a feat without falling in love completely. This was a tough life lesson, for sure.

After the auction, I planned to rely on the support of Chris, my mom, and my two mustang friends to pull me through my inevitable heartache.

My mom received another call and had to go, not a problem because my horse watched me from the pen and excitement filled me to work with her.

I dodged into the barn to feed my other horses and cow, also making up a batch of wet alpha cubes for the mustang's treat along with her pale of pellets. When I approached the pen, a sweet nicker rumbled. I was sure it had to do with the bucket of feed I carried, but I'd gladly accept her warmth. From over the fence, I dumped the contents of the bucket into the feed pan on the ground.

When she finished eating, I drew in a long breath and summoned the courage to extend my hand through the fence slats with an alfalfa cube cupped in my palm. She fixed her gaze on me as I held my position, unwavering. My arm began to tingle from holding it outward so long, but I held strong.

With this mare, nothing unfolded at a rapid pace. She excelled at testing my patience. Gradually, she took a cautious step, followed by another, until she stood just mere inches from me. The desire to reach out and touch her tempted me, but I remained still.

Her hot breath tickled my hand, filling me with excitement. I held my breath, waited, and for a fleeting moment I wondered if she planned to bite me or to take off my beloved fingers. A trace of fear coursed through me, yet at some point I needed to embrace the risk. *Have faith in the process.*

Her soft muzzle grazed my hand, and then swiftly she snatched the treat and scooted away.

I gasped, taken aback by her sheer speed, but she touched me! Even though it wasn't technically our first touch, initiated by me, it held significance. I repeated the process once more, this time requiring less demand for my patience, as she approached me quicker and mouthed the treat with more care. I set a new goal for today of feeding her a treat from inside the pen.

I pushed away from the fence, ready to start from where we left off yesterday. Picking up the liberty whips lying near the gate, I entered the ring with keen attention to the horse's body language.

She watched me but didn't move from her spot. Progress. She seemed more relaxed today, and it only required two gentle reminders to respect the liberty whips before she trotted in circles around me as I asked. She kept her inner ear trained on me for cues but respected my space, making me feel better about my goal of touching her today. If it wasn't for the dreaded timeline lingering in my mind, I'd wait and take things slower. Training took time, but lucky for me, today I felt positive, encouraged, and driven.

To break the monotony of our routine, I set aside the liberty sticks in case I later needed them for protection. I stepped from the enclosure to offer us both a well-deserved respite. The winter sun, although mild, threatened to overheat me in my winter getup, so I switched out my coat for a vest. With gratitude for Chris's insistence on buying me the cowgirl hat and was thankful for the shade on my face that it provided.

 The mare watched me as I picked up the shorter stick with the ball on the end. Not willing to step inside the pen for this activity, I poked it between the slats of the fence. She turned her head away, but I held the stick steadfast to avoid frightening her. I summoned more patience and waited. This training step served as a prelude to touching her. She cast a glance backward, and eventually, her curiosity won as she moved a few strides closer. I wanted to yelp with excitement but refrained to avoid causing her to spook.

 She paused, took two more steps, hesitated. With each movement, she swished her tail. Training her took more perseverance than I expected.

 Instead of creeping the final short distance to me, she stretched out her neck and nuzzled the ball for a split second. As if it zapped her, she spun around and scooted across the pen.

 "You're a brave girl, beautiful." My heart swelled and I mentally performed a little happy dance at her slight progress.

 I continued to hold the stick and ball in place without moving. She licked her lips in thought, and then alternated her attention between the ball and me before she inched forward. I held my breath as she reached out and touched it for a split second, but this time she didn't run away. Between fear and interest, she soaked up knowledge. I bent down and fished out a soaked alfalfa cube and held out my palm.

 Food motivated as she was, she closed the distance between us and snatched the treat before scooting off.

 Throughout the day we practiced this newfound skill. When I felt comfortable enough to attempt to feed her from inside the pen, I picked up one of the liberty whips and entered. She had no issues sharing the space with me anymore if I kept my distance, although

I planned to challenge her comfort zone. After all, today I planned to achieve our first touch. While I stood in the center of the pen for more space, I held out the whip to establish a boundary. My heart pounded as I leaned forward with my outstretched, shaky hand.

Breathe, don't let her know I'm concerned.

To lessen the intensity of the situation, I shifted my glance toward Elvis pecking at the grass in the distance. Curious by my lack of attention toward her, the horse crept closer but respected the presence of the liberty whip as a boundary. I returned my gaze to her before she stretched out her neck and, to my delight, a puff of warmth danced across my hand as she sniffed my fingers for the briefest moment. I might consider that our first touch, but barely. I retreated, using the release of pressure as a reward.

She didn't expect me to walk away and followed me toward the gate. When I swiveled slowly around on the heels of my boots, she dashed off. I had messed up again. I went too far, too fast. Those unwanted, familiar words of defeat hammered away at my mind.

Who do you think you are to train a wild horse? You aren't a trainer. Go back to nursing where you belong. She isn't going to let you touch her today, or ever. Turn her over to someone who knows what they are doing.

I tried to shrug off the horrible thoughts, tried to remain positive. I stayed inside the round pen and reached under the fence to dip my hand into the bucket for a treat, counting on food to motivate her.

Keep going, Haley. No one is going to do this for you.

Another treat piqued her interest, and she inched her way toward me. *Come on, girl.* I didn't dare speak the words out loud for fear she'd run off. When she remained still, I reached forward with my hand to offer the treat, holding the whip between us. I imagined her warm, soft coat beneath my fingertips and wanted to touch her more than I desired a hot shower tonight.

She crept closer, but when I stretched out that last little bit to offer the treat, she turned her head away from me. It made more sense to allow her to approach me. I paused, but with the speed of a bullet she struck out at me with her front leg, almost clipping my hand. I jumped, my breath catching in my throat. Like a flash of light, she bolted.

Just breathe. One breath at a time, in and out.

She had come so close to hurting me. I forced myself to remain inside the pen. I shouldn't reward her with my departure, but to be honest, I stayed mostly because my feet remained frozen in place as I caught my breath. I gripped the liberty whip to pulsate the air if she came back at me.

I repeat, do not leave this pen, Haley. It is not okay for her to charge me. Be a leader. Be a trainer.

She was just as afraid of me as I was of her.

The frightened mare stood at the farthest point from me, her head turned, blotting me out of her existence. I glanced up at the sky, the bright fireball promising an impending sunset within the next hour or so. I had come so close to our first touch, and then it passed us by like a storm cloud. My heart physically ached, and I questioned the likelihood of her ever allowing me to touch her. Kentucky seemed impossible right about now.

Not willing to give up, I reached underneath the fence to grab the second liberty whip, needing two for this activity, and started over with the original exercise of moving her around to establish boundaries. She responded well, so I decided to give us both a break and leave the round pen. It was as good time as any to feed my livestock before the sun set. Life on a farm never stopped.

The crisp air rode in with the first hint of streaked neon yellow and a fiery hue of peach across the horizon. I shivered and switched my vest out for the warmth of my winter coat. I saved feeding the mare for last, but my original idea of feeding her from a bucket while I stood inside the pen sounded ridiculous and a bit crazy. I had lost my confidence and decided to wait until I recovered from the scare and had built more trust between us. No way did I want to challenge her protective instincts for food again without a fence barrier between us.

Tossing hay into her pen, I slid the rubber pan with her dinner underneath the fence. To my dismay, she pinned her ears at me before sticking her nose into the feed. Her behavior shouldn't hurt my feelings, but it did. I longed to connect with her, longed to touch her. The annoying, logical side of my brain made me wonder if achieving such an accomplishment proved to myself that my training methods worked.

The sweet smell of pellets and fresh hay filled the air, crunching sounds narrowing the space between us as the mare scarfed her feed. My own belly rumbled as I thought about the savory beef stew marinating in the slow cooker.

I wanted to give up on this disheartening day.

The mare moved closer to me to munch at the small pile of hay.

I leaned on the fence while she mouthed the last remnants from the dirt, then she turned her attention on me. With ears perked my way, head lowered, she approached me with slow, deliberate steps. I imagined her thinking, *Why doesn't this woman leave me alone, and why does she hover by the fence to watch me eat? Doesn't she have better things to do?*

No, there was nothing more important right now than her. Our lives, Chris's and mine, revolved around the mare and the mustang makeover.

I didn't move, just focused on breathing slow and easy, riding out whatever she wanted to happen.

She crept closer, her nose jutted toward me in a friendly manner. I didn't want to mess up another possible opportunity, so I remained still. I had my arms looped through the metal rung of the fence. She paused in front of me and extended her neck, her muzzle mere inches from me. The slightest hint of hot breath blew across my arm, and the tiniest, softest touch brushed against my hand. She touched *me*! As if that weren't the best reward ever, a velvet kiss nuzzled my fingers.

The thrill of her touch overrode the fear of her chomping my hand.

With a measured patience that had fast become my motto lately, I opened my fingers with slow ease. She rested the tip of her muzzle in my palm and didn't move away when my index finger grazed the tip of her nose. It was as if she needed the touch as much as I did. I added another finger in my caress and then two more. Gratitude and appreciation for the embrace overwhelmed me, and I cherished the amount of trust she placed literally in my hands.

This was what dreams were made of.

I marveled at how miracles seem to happen when I found patience and held strong.

Keeping my touch light and gentle, I slid my hand up the bridge of her nose and rubbed her soft face. Her fur reminded me of a warm, fuzzy blanket just pulled from the dryer. Tingles ran through my hand and throughout my body as we physically connected for the first time. Not only did she let me touch her, but she allowed me to rub the precious star on that sweet forehead of hers. She leaned into me for a moment, and then poof. She was gone.

At least she hadn't scurried away, but strolled.

Chris sidled up to me at the fence. "You touched her." He grinned wide. The golden hue of the setting sun danced in his hair, making him look almost angelic. He'd probably set out to find me when I wasn't in the kitchen sampling our flavorful dinner.

"The first time." I returned his grin, my heart practically smiling that he had witnessed this amazing moment. "What time is it?" I wanted to log it in my mind forever.

"Six forty-five."

I had rubbed her face at six 6:45 p.m. on our fourth day of the makeover.

We stood in awed silence before I broke it.

"Chris, we are so far behind everyone else. Don't get me wrong, I'm grateful she let me rub her face." I hated to turn a precious moment into a negative one, but I believed in facing reality. "I don't know how we'll be ready for Kentucky."

He took hold of my hand, his touch comforting as he rubbed his thumb across the backside of my fingers. The same ones the mare had just touched. "One day at a time, Haley. That's all you can do."

"I know. Little steps make big ones." He was right and I needed to keep believing in myself and the mare.

The next morning while I fed the animals, my phone beeped with an incoming text from Lisa.

You won't believe what just happened!

I pressed my eyes closed for a moment because I knew what she wanted to tell me. I didn't want to be like that, comparing myself to others. I really didn't, so I shoved the negative thoughts away.

What happened?

I got the tag off Magnolia! Yes, that's her name.

I stepped toward the round pen and, feeling resigned, rested my arms against the fence. My mare happily chewed her hay and ignored me, so I spoke to her as I would a friend. "Did you hear that Lisa removed the tag off her mare and now she has a name? Do you want a name?" The mare lifted her head to listen but continued to chew the bits poking from her mouth. "Okay, I'll take that as you're tired of being nameless. You need to let me remove your tag."

MEET THE SPOOK HEAD-ON

Paw Paw used to say, "Comparing yourself to others undermines self-respect." Now that I've experienced training a wild mustang firsthand, I grasped a deeper meaning of his wise words.

I kept thinking about the text exchange with Lisa. Difficult as it might be, I wish I didn't compare myself to how far the other trainers in the program had progressed. I had experienced too many challenges with my mustang to let myself feel inferior by the lack of headway. No one judged me, nor should I.

My phone beeped again.

Guess what else happened?

Trepidation gripped me but Lisa expected an answer back to her text. I held my phone in my hand. I did wish my friends the best, I just needed to step measuring myself against what others accomplished.

I paused before texting back to ponder what to name my own mare. At first, I had thoughts about calling her Beast, or some equally intimidating name, but she deserved something sweet, something that reminded me of her heritage.

"We're going to work on the tag thing," I said as she ignored me. "It's coming. You can snub reality all you want." When she didn't acknowledge my voice, I turned my attention back to my phone to text Lisa.

Tell me. What else happened?

I was happy for her, really.

I sat on her for the first time!

My world stilled. Lisa sat on Magnolia. Certainly, my complicated, envious emotions were normal, weren't they? I worked endless hours a day to connect with this wild mare. Our first touch felt minimized compared to this news. I don't know how I thought we'd be ready to compete against experienced trainers.

I shook my head. *Do not minimize your success, Haley. Each horse is different.*

Chin held high, I texted her back.

Oh, wow! Congrats! That is huge.

I kept my own good news about rubbing the mare's face to myself.

One good thing came from the text exchange. Her news forced me to push myself outside my comfort zone. Kentucky required more than simply rubbing the mare's face. It demanded I ride her inside a huge arena with noisy people and awful acoustics. My dream of performing without a bridle and saddle in our championship freestyle class to synchronized music still lived inside of me, so I needed to step up my game.

"We can do this," I said to my horse. She lifted her head and a low rumble escaped her throat. I gulped, straining to hear the noise again. "Did you nicker?"

Another muted sound rewarded my heart, so faint I questioned if my imagination played tricks on me. I was fairly certain I heard right.

"Good girl. That's so much better than a snort."

Prompted by my words, she strolled over to the fence but didn't allow me to touch her.

"We're going to power up today, Ms. Mare."

Not only did I plan to touch her again while inside the round pen, but I also set a goal to lead her with a rope attached to the halter she already wore, thanks to Lisa. With that in mind, I entered the enclosure and let her come to me. I attempted to rub her face, but no matter how I tried, or how slow I went, she refused to allow me to touch any part of her. I drove her away with the liberty whips and into a canter to make her work. There was truth to the one step forward, twenty steps backward notion.

Time was of the essence. She watched as I hurried to the barn to retrieve a lead rope. When I hustled back to the pen, she spooked, reacting to the wild person running at her, meaning me. I slowed down for a moment to placate her, then changed my mind.

Meet the spook head-on, Haley. Invariably we needed practice for the inevitable noises and movement sure to greet us in the vast arena at the competition. I set down my training tools, glad no one was around to witness my plan, and then I let loose with all my pent-up tension. I ran in circles around the outside of the pen, swinging my arms in the air. I yelled out random, positive words and sentences, such as *we are the world, we can do anything, whoop, whoop.* I jumped around and laughed, then laughed more. Stored-up stress poured out through my laughter. Boy, I must be loony but this was fun. I bent over and laughed harder, even snorted.

When I stopped, gasping for breath, I glanced up to take in the surprised expression on her face. She wrinkled her brows, lifted her head into the air, and flipped her lip upward as if laughing with me. Her response initiated another round of merriment. I had been too concerned before to relax, but it was past time to include playful fun into our training regimen. It dawned on me that we were experiencing a bonding moment.

Lisa's text had been the catalyst for my new outlook on training my mustang, and I thanked her in silence.

I entered the pen. "Let's try leading with a rope, girl." She allowed me to touch the rope halter without a fuss, just not her face. "There's no time like the present." The staff member had been right about forcing the issue of having her wear a halter.

The best strategy remained to let her approach me. Feigning nonchalance, I strolled away from her with the lead rope draped over my shoulder, a liberty whip in hand, mostly for communication purposes instead of concern for my safety, not giving her an ounce of attention. She didn't expect my behavior and became curious. The shuffling dirt sounded behind me, and I knew she followed, but I ignored her and kept walking while wearing a grin.

When I stopped in place to test her attentiveness, a thump to my back about knocked me over, causing me to giggle without her spooking.

Using the liberty whip, I asked for her to back up out of my space. Out of respect for the boundary that I set, she moved backward, except she did flick her tail with resistance. I let that go for now. Pleased by her progress, I stood still to let her rest as a reward and temptation to touch her gnawed at me. Oh, how I wanted to rub that star.

"You're okay, beautiful. I'm not going to hurt you."

I glanced at the imposing tag that haunted me in my dreams at night. I imagined all sorts of dangerous reactions when I removed it and hoped none came true. Sometimes my dreams were more positive, and I held the removed tag in my hand. Wanting the latter scenario, I reached out to touch the tag as it dangled from around her neck by a rope. Unfortunately, she overreacted and bolted away, kicking out too close for comfort, but not at me directly. I stood still in the blowing dust with full appreciation of her power, her strength. The fear remained real, knowing if she wanted to, she could hurt me … or worse.

The fight-or-flight mode kicked in whenever she experienced fear. Her behavior consisted of either running off or charging like a bull and, if given a choice, scooting away remained loads easier to deal with and safer than facing aggression.

I had no choice but to remain in the pen to avoid rewarding her for the unwanted behavior. Instead, I put her to work, making her canter around me in the ring, telling her what direction to go instead of her dictating my steps. I offered her a rest and reattempted to touch her, only retreating when the approach went well.

The technique worked like a charm. She followed me wherever I strolled, eventually sniffing the air between us but not allowing me to touch her. I held onto my patience, tapping into some of the same skills I used with my patients at the hospital when needed. It was a bit disappointing, though. I had thought that since I had touched her last night, she'd let me touch her again without an issue.

Nothing was easy with this mare.

While glancing at the tag, I noticed a worn spot on her fur from where the halter rubbed her face. The first opportunity the mare allowed, I needed to change out the small halter for a larger one. While I looked forward to removing the tag and finally giving her a name, I can't say I looked forward to the task of changing out the halters, even though I moved it high up on my priority list.

We practiced leading without the rope attached, and she learned I stored treats in my coat pocket. Feeding horses rewards as a technique remained a topic of controversy in the training world, but right now I had a short deadline and a difficult horse. To my relief, by the end of the day she allowed me to lead her with an attached rope to her halter around the pen.

When we stopped to rest, I finagled the halter and pulled it downward, holding onto it until she lowered her head. She licked her lips with thought, so I released to reward. Teaching her to give into pressure had many benefits, such as transferring over to when I rode her. Sitting on her back seemed almost impossible to imagine with all the work left ahead of us.

"Good girl. We've got this. You and me, we're a team."

I embraced my philosophy of earning her trust, earning her willingness to want to please me.

Touching the tag, feeling its glorious cool metal, I held it in my hand for a long, wonderful moment. When she ripped away without warning and ran off to the opposite side of the pen, her reaction left me taken aback. I was so close to possibly removing it, to being able to name her, that my stomach churned. I didn't want to end the day on a sour note and wished I had stopped before attempting to touch the tag, but lesson learned. Every step forward took a hundred times longer than what I expected. My heart sank, literally hurt at the sad thought of her fate if I failed to train her in time for Kentucky.

Somehow, I had to break through the horse's overall fear of humans and teach her to trust. Not easy to do with less than ninety days left.

THE LASSO

I held to the belief that the heart of a horse yearned to connect with a human—mind, body, and soul. I remembered what Paw Paw had told me about the horse being good for the inside of a man, or in this case, a woman.

"You can do this," Chris had said to me one night when I had forgotten the "why" in all of this. "When you feel down, just remember your childhood when you rode your horse with your hands in the air. You convinced me you were meant for this program because your lifelong dream was to train a wild mustang. Hold on to that passion, Haley."

My spirit had needed that lift.

This chilly morning, I felt revived, ready to start a new day of training. If anyone had the ability to help this mare, it was me because I cared about her.

Today's plan focused on leading and fine-tuning halter pressure to increase the communication between us. Bigger yet, I wanted to tackle removing the menacing tag, a constant reminder of my inadequacies. Though I tried not to compare myself to my fellow online mustang trainers, I kept doing exactly that. The weight of knowing I remained the only one who failed to remove the tag jabbed at me. The disappointment felt like someone driving five steel tines of a pitchfork into my self-esteem.

While I watched my mare munch hay, I noticed the rubbed place on her face had turned raw. Exchanging the halter today became critical. This gave me added incentive to address both the halter exchange and the removal of the tag in one fell swoop. I'd be dishonest if I didn't admit my edgy nerves practically clung to a cliff's edge at the mere thought, but I needed to earmark the day for tackling looming tasks.

When the mustang finished eating, I entered the pen, grateful she allowed me to now walk up to her without issue. She pivoted around to greet me with a nicker and kind eyes. She took a treat from my hand.

"Good morning, beautiful. I've been thinking about names for you." Positive names, I might add.

I waited for her curiosity to kick in at my outstretched arm and threatless hand, for her to sniff or touch me, but she tuned me out. Being patient, I remained still, imagining how coarse her long mane would feel if I ran my fingers in her tangled hair, jet black, thick, and wild, flopped on each side of her neck.

Keeping my energy light, I tinkered with the rope knot that held the halter in place, then released my contact as a reward. The exchange needed to happen first due to its priority status caused by the rubbed spot on her face, but the thought of the halter sliding off if she moved during the swap scared me, as it was an integral form of communication between us.

I worked with her intermittently for the next several hours, taking mental rest breaks for both of us while I finished barn chores. Things went smoothly until Elvis strutted toward the round pen with his long black and white feathers fanned out wide. He gobbled in arrogance at the mare and dove under the fence as he'd done the first morning after we'd brought the mare home.

She pinned her ears and charged, almost trampling him. I had experienced firsthand that sense of utter vulnerability and had empathy for him.

"Elvis, get out of there," I commanded. The turkey ignored me, strutting back and forth near the fence line to taunt her. Then striding after the mare, he made his threatening *blbblbbb* noises. Since he hadn't learned his lesson, she bared her teeth and shot toward him, sending Elvis running underneath the fence before she was able to squash him. He continued to gobble and taunt her from the safety of the other side. The dude was fearless, facing her straight on like that. I preferred the subtle but firm approach, as I valued my life.

The mare jutted her nose at him and snorted. I swear a plume of steam puffed into the cold air, as if a raging bull prepared to charge through the fence. A loud snort echoed in the country silence. She stuck her nose through a fence slat and huffed a forceful breath. The prideful booger didn't move and had the audacity to peck her nose. She jumped in place, stunned the little guy nabbed her.

Even though I found Elvis scary, I wanted to protect my horse. "Elvis, go on. Scram." I swayed my arms in the air, but he ignored me. He pecked at her again but didn't make contact. Unsatisfied, he whirled around in attempt to accost me. *Blbbbb bllbbbbb.* A high-pitch warning trailed to a lower tone but strung out like the screech of brakes. Whoever labeled it as "gobble" glorified the reverberating noise.

I stomped my foot, making myself big as I had learned with the mare. If I could handle an eleven-hundred-pound horse, a sassy turkey … no problem. I slammed my foot to the ground again and swung my arms over my head like a wild woman, then closed the distance between us with swift movements. The mare took off and ran to the far side of the pen, but the blasted turkey retaliated with a *blbbb.*

I closed the gap between us—a week ago I'd never dare attempt this—and swung my arms more. "Leave her alone. You mess with my horse, dude, you mess with me. Got that, Elvis?"

He sassed me, his hair still fluffed, but he strutted off to hang out with his duck friend by the silo.

Wondering where the dogs were through all of this, I glanced around the farm, but they were nowhere to be found. My guess was they had followed Chris to the back field.

"Enough procrastination," I said to the mare, who watched

me in amazement. I swear she knew I stood up to that intimidating turkey to protect her. "I have your back, girl. We hold the world in our hands." I flexed my biceps. "And I *am* a real trainer." What freedom I felt saying those words aloud.

I approached her, took hold of the precious halter with a whole new level of confidence, and played with it with minimal reaction from her. "We're going to change this out today, so it doesn't continue to hurt you."

She bent her neck around to nuzzle me. I laughed and rubbed my hand just behind her ears. She sidestepped to evade my touch, but I used the pressure-release technique with the halter until she lowered her head.

I left the pen, first glancing around to check the whereabouts of Elvis. Coast clear, I hurried to the training barn to retrieve a larger halter. When I returned to the pen, the mare waited for me at the gate for the first time, causing me to swallow hard from the emotion welling up inside me.

"I thought of the perfect name for you, but I can't call you it until we get this tag off," I said in the soothing voice she had come to recognize. I hadn't even shared the name with Chris yet. I envisioned a name that captured the essence of who she was as a horse, her history, her heritage. "If that isn't motivation to remove the tag, I don't know what is."

Her soft nicker made my day.

We spent the next hour improving pressure and release techniques with the halter and rubbing circles near her ears. She needed to accept my touch without reaction, horses often being sensitive about their ears being touched, to prepare her for the exchange. It also seemed as good a time as any to play more with the tag.

"Winners don't quit," I said more to myself than to her while rubbing her face. She studied me with interest.

I worked my way behind her ears again, and eventually she allowed me to rub the back of them with what I assumed was acceptance.

Knowing better than to push my luck, my impatience won out to exchange the halters and to possibly remove the tag. If all went well, I planned to take a long lunch to enjoy my delicious chicken and rice leftovers as my own reward.

With her head lowered, I rubbed the new halter over her face to desensitize her further. If I had done the training right, I should have all the time in the world to switch them, but my fear of her running off scared me. I wrapped a lead rope around her neck to give me something else to hold onto if needed. Inhaling a long breath to calm my nerves, I loosened the knot of the tight halter the staff member had secured on her face. I wished I had three hands right now.

I tried to move fast. I let the old halter trail down my arm and cradled it with my elbow, then rubbed her face and slid the new one up her nose. When it came time to pull the rope behind her ears, she walked in circles around me. I held on as if my life depended on this task.

If I lost her, then I'd have bigger problems. The communication the halter offered remained crucial, and we'd be set back a good week or two if she ran off. We didn't have that kind of free time.

She stopped in place, lifted her head, and I tied the rope halter before she scooted to the side. I traveled with her and double-checked the knot. It felt secure to me, and I only hoped that was the case. I decided not to tackle the removal of the tag just yet.

I refrained from jumping up and down to celebrate, wanting to end on a calm note. *Oh my gosh, I changed out the halter!* Mission completed.

"Good girl!"

I unwrapped the lead rope from her neck, handed her a treat, then practically ran to the house to eat a late lunch. My pace caught the dogs' attention. They bolted across the barnyard toward me, barking and wanting to play. When they reached me, I patted them both on the head before I beelined inside with Stubby at my heels. Ringo stayed behind in the carport as usual.

Not wanting to take the precious few minutes to heat up the chicken, I scarfed it down cold, devouring every bite including a second helping. When my allotted lunchbreak ended too soon, my intuition nudged me to peek out the window to check on the mare. There she stood, in the center of the round pen, without a halter.

My breath caught in my throat. *No!* This couldn't be happening.

I almost vomited my lunch but managed to talk myself into breathing deeper. It worked for a moment before I glanced at the mare again.

I grabbed my coat and shoved my arms through the arm holes as I ran outside. A simple sprint across the yard was nothing right now, and I paid no attention to Elvis chasing me with his feathers splayed outward. I hurried toward the mare. She spooked and began running around, and chaos ensued. Elvis made his threatening noises and scurried in circles, all of us flustered. There, lying in a heap on the dirt, the halter mocked me. The mare stopped running, watching me as if laughing too.

Really? I mean come on. How had the blasted thing fallen off? I thought I had tied it well. Then again, my hands had been full of ropes, and I had hurried to prevent her from spinning. Whatever the reason, the halter was now coiled in a bundle on the ground.

My mind twirled, overwhelmed. What now, and how to fix this unfortunate situation?

She refused to let me touch her without a halter, nor allowing me anywhere near her. The mare realized she was free.

We were almost back to the beginning of her training. Without a halter and lead rope, an artificial aide I had never wanted to rely on in the first place, I had lost direct contact without a way to communicate with her effectively. I fought off rising panic.

Breathe in, breathe out.

This couldn't be the end of our training. I just needed to figure out a way around this snafu.

Think.

I snapped my fingers as a thought circulated through my mind. Chris kept a lasso in the training barn. That was it, the answer. I would rope her myself. I had a friend in high school who taught me how to swing and throw a lasso.

Though I was no rodeo queen!

I glanced at the mare, determined to fix my mistake, willing to give the lasso experiment a shot.

I rushed toward the barn and retrieved Chris's lariat from a rusted hook, then grabbed a pair of worn work gloves from the seat of the tractor before hurrying back to the pen. All the while the mare watched me with interest, knowing her crazy human was up to foolish shenanigans again.

Here came Elvis, fluffed up and striding toward me. In all the upset, I had forgotten about him.

"Oh, no you don't. I have more important things to focus on besides dealing with you." I stomped at him, but he continued to accost me, making those threatening non-gobble noises. "Get out of here."

He didn't leave. I tossed the lasso at him, wanting him to back off, but my action made him more aggressive. "Go find your duck girlfriend," I commanded.

Blbbbb.

I strode past him, aware that he strutted after me. I whirled around. With a surprising level of confidence, I stepped toward him, waving my hands above my head.

He ran off. "Don't come back," I called after him.

When I returned to the round pen, I bent over and laughed at myself, glad no one witnessed the Elvis drama.

The mare stared at me. "You're next, my friend." I held the coils in my left hand, with the tail of the rope on my left side. The loop rested in my right hand with an arm's length of slack between, just as my friend had taught me. I practiced swinging the loop across my body first, making sure the bottom strand flipped across my wrist. My friend's words echoed in my mind as she mentally guided me. When I had the technique down, I moved to swinging the loop above my head, making sure to keep my palm facing down to avoid entanglement. All the new activity caused the mare to race around the pen, head held high, nostrils flared, snorting.

Better to desensitize her before I tried to lasso her. It had been at least two years since I'd picked up the lariat, other than to move it out of my way. Swinging the loop was awkward at first. I aimed at a large stone, following through as I released the rope, but the loop landed nowhere near where I'd hoped.

My arm throbbed from swinging around the lasso, and I needed to feed the animals their dinner before I tackled roping my horse. Who knew how long that might take? In anticipation of the mare running around during the lasso activity, I decided not to feed her until after we finished to keep from upsetting her tummy.

Taking my time, I doled out feed for my other animals. Junior, my favorite old horse, nickered at me. "Why can't the mustang be happy to see me like you are?" He nickered again in answer as I dumped his feed in his bucket. It didn't take long to care for the rest of the animals, and I stopped to rest a moment to prepare myself for the challenge that awaited me.

I suspected it might take a while to lasso her.

When I returned to the pen, she stood at the gate, waiting for her food. "Sorry, girl. Not until we finish what we started." I planned to stay up all night if that was what it took.

I picked up the lariat with silent respect for my friend, grateful she had taught me what little I knew. Practice would make the difference between success and failure, so I kept going until my swing flowed, as well as my follow-through, and I had corrected the timing of the release.

After the rope landed where I intended several times in a row, I entered the round pen full of confidence and vigor.

Girl, if you're going to wear a hat, it's time to be that cowgirl.

The mare's eyes widened with concern. She held back against

the far fence, watching every move I made, her legs sprawled out as if trying to decide what direction to run in if I did anything spontaneous with the lariat.

I swung the loop above my head as I had practiced. When I released the rope in the air, it sailed with a wobble and thudded against her neck. She took off, bucking and kicking out at me.

Okay, so I needed a wee bit more practice. When she slowed down to a trot, evading me with her neck bent away, I swung the rope again, hitting the ground behind her. Never had I tried to rope a moving object.

Unwarranted confidence circulated through me, my determination to rope the mare manifesting beyond anything I had experienced before.

My raised arm ached in the cold weather, my face feeling chilled despite sweating. The drop in temperature did nothing to stop beads of perspiration from gathering at my neck and underneath my coat. I wished I had taken it off before I started this endeavor. When the outdoor light popped on, I realized the sun had long since disappeared beyond the dark hill, and I was about to run out of daylight.

No way could I stop now.

After several more unsuccessful swings of the loop, I stopped to catch my breath and to let her rest. It was best to avoid overworking her in the cold and making her winter coat damp. I had no idea how long I'd been out there swinging a rope, but I bent over, resting my hands on my knees. Being a cowgirl was no easy feat.

Night slipped in with a starry black cloak. A thin slice of moon watched over me, and faded twinkles in the sky refused to absorb my disappointment. Chris's truck pulled onto the grass near the round pen. The headlights beamed, light fanning out and illuminating the round pen more than the outdoor lamp I had come to rely on during late nights. I hadn't realized how low light the conditions were before he showed up.

He climbed out, pushing back his own cowboy hat, and

asked, "Haley, what are you doing?"

I walked to the fence to greet him, fighting off tears, not wanting him to witness my devastating failure. "I had to switch out the halter but it fell off." I swallowed hard, trying to clear the lump in my throat.

"And you decided to lasso her?" A slow smile spread across his face.

I nodded without speaking.

"Haley, you've never used a lasso on an animal before. She's a strong, wild mustang." His voice held humor and rang with the sharp edge of truth. "She could have hurt you, or worse."

"I know," I managed to say, knowing I wasn't doing a good job roping her.

His smile turned into a grin. "You're gonna have to do better than that if you want to catch her."

"Fine," I said, my feisty streak kicking in. "Why don't *you* come in here and rope her?"

The side of his mouth curled. He flashed me an amused nod, and I handed him the lariat.

He pulled off a cowboy gimp to return to his truck and fetched a pair of leather gloves. He practiced a few overhead swings, roped the rock I had tried so hard to lasso, and then entered the lion's den.

The mare didn't know him, so this should be an interesting adventure. I left the pen and crossed my arms to watch.

The mare snorted at him and splayed her front legs to ready herself to either run or charge him. I'd be willing to flip a quarter on that guess.

Chris swung the loop with a practiced ease that made me grit my teeth. I watched as she galloped around, Chris tossing the rope and missing for several tries until the loop landed over her neck.

She bucked with force and kicked at him. He leaned back on his heels, digging them into the dirt as she ran around the pen, dragging him like he waterskied. She viewed him as a predator. And there was the predicament, the irony, he was now attached to her by the rope. I needed to take over before the situation turned ugly.

"Let me take it from here," I said, eager to help calm her down. "She knows me."

He nodded with a grimace on his face but continued to hold onto the racing, bucking horse. When she broke to a trot, I hurried inside the pen behind him. He panted and seemed hesitant to hand her over.

"Chris, I've got this." I took the rope from him and held on.

"Mare, calm down. You're fine," I said in a soothing voice to connect with her. "We're going to take care of this halter issue."

Chris backed away and left the round pen. He watched for a few minutes, then said, "Text me if you need more help." He slowed as if he had reservations about leaving me alone with the mustang.

"Thanks, I'll be fine," I said, determined to achieve success on my own but grateful at the same time for his help. Otherwise, I might have been there late at night, swinging the lariat. Accepting his assistance, despite my stubborn will, was its own lesson.

When he pulled away, the night grew dark and quiet again.

The mare had stopped to catch her breath in the glow from the overhead light, but it wasn't long before she took off running again. I gripped the rope, grateful for my gloves. She shook her head in defiance but didn't have as much energy, therefore didn't pull on me as hard as she had Chris. Unfortunately, my arms ached, and I wanted to collapse into the dirt.

"Please, oh please. Let the fight go, Ms. Mare."

She yielded a hard buck in a silent, yet loud answer, yanking the rope free of my hands.

It was too short for me to grab from the danger zone behind her back hooves. I refused to give up, to let her spend the night terrified by the rope dragging behind her. My worst nightmare was she'd tangle her legs and break bones. No way could I sleep tonight until I haltered her. It was now or never.

Steam curled off her back in waves and floated into the cold evening air. Walking was the best remedy to cool her down, so I clicked my tongue to move her forward but kept my energy low to keep her calm.

When she halted, she lowered her neck.

"I understand. I'm exhausted too." Chris had done the muscle part, so I had to suck it up. The mare stood still so long that I assumed she had no intention of taking off again.

I stepped forward and reached underneath the fence to finger the new halter closer. The mare kept her head lowered, eyes half closed, appearing to have no fear whatsoever. Now was my chance. I sauntered toward her. No big deal, or so I hoped.

"Hey, beautiful. Let's put this on you." All I wished for right now was that she'd let me slip on the halter. No matter the late hour, I had to continue until I finished the task, despite the chill. My body begged for my soft bed, warm blankets, the comfort of Chris. But the mare came first, her training and health most important.

I took hold of the lasso hanging from around her neck, and she allowed me to rub my gloved hand over her with casual strokes. I wanted to feel her soft hair underneath my fingertips but didn't want to startle her by removing my gloves. "That's right, girl. Just relax and we'll have this halter on you in no time. Then we can both rest."

When she relaxed her neck muscles, I took that as agreement. With confidence, I slid the rope noseband over her muzzle and onto her face without issue. Pulling it around her ears was a different story. I swallowed hard, remembering how she had shed the last halter and left it in the dirt. This one needed to stay on.

The mare backed up, and I walked with her, holding the halter in place until she stopped. This was the hardest part. I bit down on my lower lip, refusing the temptation to hurry and tie the rope in place. Instead, I slipped the rope off as a reward. I wanted to train her right, and her acceptance was my plight in this training style I chose. Her opinion mattered.

We went back and forth several times, but she finally allowed me to loop the rope behind her ears. She tossed her head but chose to stand still. I squinted in the poor overhead lighting to tie the knot. This time I made darn sure it wouldn't fall off.

The metal tag stared at me as if daring me to remove it. Someone had scrawled the number 6642 in black permanent marker.

She's tired, I'm exhausted, but take advantage of the timing. Use her fatigue to my benefit.

I rubbed my fingers along the gray rope, looped around her neck like a necklace with a pendant dangling underneath. The rope ran through a small hole in the tag, and the BLM—Bureau of Land Management—had secured it by tying three snug knots after the helicopter roundup, once at the holding facility. She pulled away, but I kept my grip firm. Putting her training above my own agenda, I rewarded her by letting go but determined to remove the blasted piece of metal if it was the last thing I did tonight.

Talk about reaching a milestone that lived just beyond the removal of the tag, a new beginning. There would be no more calling her *the mare*.

I wrangled with the rope, holding on when she shook her neck to stop me from bothering her. Struggling for several long minutes, I worked this first knot free. The next knot took more finagling but eventually loosened. Just when I had one more knot to free, she spun in a circle, and I had to hustle to stay beside her. Point one for her. Thankfully, I still held onto the loop around her neck.

One step forward, twenty steps back.

I refused to give up. Time to change up the game.

Holding the lariat with a relaxed grip so she didn't feel my tension, I turned my back to her and walked away. Little by little, I fed out the rope. From my peripheral vision, I saw her raise her head in curiosity, and then she surprised me by following. A point for me in this game of tit for tat. Continuing to ignore her, I strolled around the pen as if my body didn't ache from fatigue. My belly rumbled, and despite my hunger, I kept moving.

When I halted, the horse did too. Another point for me. I was in the lead.

"Good girl." I rubbed my hand along the white spot on her face and then down her neck. "Let's get this bad boy off of you." I worked my way to the tag. When she didn't move away, I struggled with the last knot that straddled the line between frustration and freedom.

It had taken ten days to reach this milestone.

The rope freed and slipped from her neck. I paused, staring at the silver tag I'd dreamed of holding. Here it was, in my hand. My emotions surged, tears dripping from my eyes.

I glanced up at her with blurred vision. "Nevada." I enjoyed the word as it rolled off my tongue. "That's your new name."

She stared at me, our gazes meeting for a long, precious moment, bonding us unlike anything I had ever experienced. Then she sniffed the tag in my hand.

"That's right. Good girl, Nevada." The name fit her well. She had roamed the desert, the Triple B HMA (herd management area), located approximately thirty miles northwest of Ely, Nevada. By the chance of a miracle, she had found her way to me.

My next lofty goal was to sit on her bareback.

RIDE HER, COWGIRL

Today I planned to sit on Nevada. Maybe I was overconfident, but excitement swirled through my entire body. Without a doubt, I knew I would never forget this day my entire life.

I had spent long days that turned into a slow couple of weeks focused on training as I prepared Nevada for this big day. The crux of the training included rubbing her all over with different items to desensitize her, as well as leaning on her back to acclimatize her to my weight. It was no surprise to me when prepping her for riding took twenty times longer than I imagined, requiring me to break down each task into even smaller, tinier steps.

But today was the day.

Despite my anticipation, with a mere sixty days left the decreasing time frame gnawed away at my insides. It didn't seem possible for us to catch up with the other trainers and, as usual, I was the only one who hadn't ridden my horse yet. I don't know why I cared so much about what other trainers thought, but I did.

Leaning against the metal fence in my usual position as Nevada munched hay, I marveled at her beauty. Hints of a stunning buckskin color showed underneath thick patches of shedding hair. If I were an outsider judging her on appearance alone, I might mistake her for a neglected, forgotten beast with a mangy coat and wild mane. She was anything but forgotten, as I loved her dearly and saw the hint of a kitten inside that untamed lion. I had to keep believing in Nevada, to keep believing in my mission of gentling her while maintaining her spirit.

I still held a mixed opinion about the roundups, the helicopter gathers, the holding pens, so I had decided to dig deeper into the hot topic. From what I understood, if horses lacked ample pasture to graze, such as the low-rainfall predicament of a desert, the horses unintentionally ripped up the entire root system of grass. However, I found it interesting to learn cows wrap their tongues around the grass to eat and cause less damage. To the contrary, horse manure makes better fertilizer for the grass than cow manure.

To further complicate the argument of allowing the wild horses to remain on the public lands, some said the management group held more interest in earning money to lease the vast land to cattle ranchers. Sufficient drinking water remained a huge issue. Ranchers made money off their livestock; therefore, they had resources to provide their own water source if needed. No one provided this luxury for the wild horses because no one owned them. It hurt my heart to think of an animal searching for water in a hot desert.

The roundups had been a heated topic for a while now. Horse advocates state the helicopters caused stress among the horses and indicated occasional injuries or fatalities. They wanted to find a gentler solution to the roundups, or a different birth control method altogether, so the mustangs were able to remain free to roam the land. I had seen disheartening footage online to support both viewpoints.

I understood the different stances on this complex issue and tried to avoid heated debates. The way I figured, the roundups continued to happen despite the controversy, but at least the makeover provided an opportunity for the horses to leave the holding pens and have a chance for adoption. In my humble opinion all horses, captured or domestic, deserved a loving home. No matter one's belief on the tumultuous subject, the horses in captivity required help.

Today, I planned to help Nevada by taking the next required

step in preparation for Kentucky. When she finished her hay, I rubbed her all over with my hand first, and then a tarp. I used the liberty whips to direct her movement in the round pen, along with more desensitization protocols. Next, I used an oversized squishy ball to rub along her body and to drape across her back, as well as using a bareback pad for riding. It took more patience on my part to wait for her to accept the scary tarp I placed on the ground and over her back. I even placed a western saddle on her so someone else could eventually ride her. Progress remained slow but steady.

If I were able to set my own pace without a deadline, I'd wait longer to sit on her, but I had done most everything I could think of to prepare her. I found it next to impossible to avoid comparing myself to my friends who had progressed to not only riding their mares, but to steering them over obstacles and adventuring out on short trail rides. At times I had to pull myself out of bouts of negative beliefs of inadequacy, but I showed up daily and tried my best.

Today, right now, I faced my own mix of hesitation combined with excitement. It was time to mount Nevada. I swore someone had their hand squeezed around my throat, making it difficult to breathe.

I secured my trusty helmet, stepped onto the mounting block, and swallowed hard. *Breathe in long breaths ... let them out slower.*

Still holding on to my desire to ride her bareback without a bridle and saddle at the competition, I planned to sit on her first without the saddle. I couldn't wait to feel her warmth underneath me, to connect with her on a personal level.

I tied a thick rope around Nevada's neck to hold but used no bridle or halter. The rope seemed less invasive, less like entrapment for Nevada, plus I envisioned I could slip off her back in a hurry without getting tangled in the reins or having a saddle in the way. I had my mind set on training her a certain way and wanted to do everything myself.

Nevada waited with patience for me to get over myself and

my annoying apprehension. She knew to stand still, as I had leaned over her countless times while resting my full weight against her. I sucked in one more long breath. Now was the precious moment I had dreamed about.

I swallowed hard, relieved that Chris worked in the shop nearby if I needed him.

Talk to her. It will relax you both.

"Nevada, we've been through it all, so you know I won't hurt you. Be gentle." I rubbed my hand on her and grabbed a chunk of her thick black mane. Splaying myself across her back, in slow motion, I swung my right leg around to the opposite side of her body. All seemed good, so I sat up in one long, slow motion.

I fought off tears of joy and blinked hard. Here I was, sitting atop a broad Nevada mountain, feeling like a resilient warrior princess who had won a grueling battle. I rubbed her with my hand, both of us having earned this reward for putting in long, difficult days. What a gift, to connect with a mare who had no intention to bond initially.

She turned her nose toward my knee and sniffed, as if wondering how I had ended up perched on her back. I shifted slightly to adjust my balance, but her back tensed underneath me. Clearly, she didn't realize I might move while sitting on her.

She bolted forward like a racehorse leaving the gate. What power! I knotted my hands into her mane when I started to slip. The rodeo buck underneath me shook my soul, then her exaggerated leap caused me to grip with my thighs to stay on her back. She lowered her neck, feet off the ground more than they touched. The sheer rocket force caused me to squeeze with my legs, terrified of dying.

The strand of her mane ripped from my grasp. She ducked her head, kicked out with forceful vibrance, and sent me sailing over her ears. Time froze in one long, chilling moment. My life paused midair. Then, with an agonizing thump, the hard dirt greeted me. My mind blanked as the air gushed from my lungs.

Where was I? What happened?

I struggled to catch my jagged breath, inhaling as if someone smothered me with a pillow. Fiery pain shot throughout my body, so I lay perfectly still in my sorrow.

I had failed.

Nevada planted herself at the farthest point of the pen, snorting at me. Didn't she recognize me splayed out in a lump on the dirt? Things had gone wrong fast.

I tried to drag in long breaths, enough to scream to Chris, and it took everything I had. On the count of three I would yell for him. One, two ... three.

"Chris ... help." It came out as a squeak, so I dragged in the biggest breath possible and managed to yell louder.

Silence greeted me, so I remained still as a limp noodle, my head resting on my arm, my ego lying in the dirt next to me.

I had no faith left. Maybe I wasn't a horse trainer. My friends were trail riding and enjoying their horses, and here I was, drowning in failure. The pressure of Kentucky cornered me.

Once again, I wondered how I possibly thought training a wild mustang was my calling.

I glanced up at Nevada. Our gazes met in one long, still moment.

She watched me. I watched her.

My body ached, and my eyelids grew heavy as if tiny weights were attached to them. I shut my eyes, fighting consciousness.

A scrambling noise pierced my internal dark world, but I kept my eyes shut, unsure if Nevada planned to trample me or if Chris ran toward me. The gate clicked open, then shut, and shuffling dirt noises and feet scurried my way. Nevada barely knew Chris other than the experience of his lasso landing around her neck. Her snort rang through the air, and I opened my eyes to witness her trotting back and forth from the safety of her designated side of the pen. I hoped she didn't charge him, or we'd both be in a bad predicament. My protective instincts for Chris kicked in, not that I was able to help him.

"Oh, my gosh, Haley." He kneeled beside me and took hold

of my hand. "Do I need to call an ambulance?"

I shook my head without speaking, words too much an effort. What an alarming thought to have an ambulance escort me to the hospital, the place of my employment—*no, thank you*—with my coworkers discovering my failed dream to train horses.

"If you need to go, don't talk yourself out of it." Chris read my mind.

"I'm okay," I whispered. I had no medical proof to back up the claim, but because Chris was near me, I already felt better. The pain in my body dulled, my headache faded, but my pride … *ouch*.

I grabbed hold of his arm to sit but he stopped me.

"Don't rush. Take your time." The tender way he spoke meant my fall scared him half to death. Ditto. It terrified me.

The ground had a way of feeling like concrete when a horse launched you onto it. My mind spun around, so I closed my eyes until the dizzy wave passed.

When I opened them, blinking twice to clear my vision, Chris leaned over me. The tight lines on his forehead made me feel guilty for scaring him. I swear he aged ten years from seeing me on the ground.

Movement from the corner of my eye caught my attention. Despite her apprehension about Chris, Nevada crept closer with her head lowered, nostrils flared. She stopped a few feet away, splaying her front legs like a newborn foal, and snorted.

"Nevada, it's just me." I resisted the urge to stand up and console her, but the fact she cared enough to approach me filled my heart with love.

Pulling on Chris's arm, I struggled to sit. My motion sent Nevada spinning in a complete circle before darting off to her safe place in the pen.

"Sweetheart, are you okay?"

"Umm. Think so." Breathing became easier now that I sat up, but I didn't feel like chatting.

"Are you able to stand?"

I shrugged but let him help me up slowly. My body swayed,

and I needed to stand still to allow my vision to clear, but hey, I was on my feet.

"In the house to rest, Haley."

I shook my head to protest, but he didn't give me a choice. He led me to the gate while supporting me with his arm around my waist.

"What about the rope around her neck?" I asked. "I ... don't ... want her to get tangled." Conversation remained a struggle, and my energy drained from me like an overturned cup.

He guided me to Nevada so I could remove the rope, keeping his hand on my waist. Nevada eyed Chris but stretched her neck out and nuzzled my elbow. I swear she wanted to apologize for bucking me off. I patted her for reassurance and removed the rope. "No hard feelings, girl."

The folds above her eyes wrinkled with concern. My emotions spiked, and I fought off tears of failure. I had to believe we had what it took to make it to Kentucky.

"Have faith, Haley." Chris held onto me as I removed the rope.

Have faith. His words echoed through me.

We made our way to the house, but what I had said to Nevada didn't ring true. I did have hard feelings, but not toward her. I hid deep inside me an unsurmountable amount of anger, along with embarrassment and a sense of failure for apparently skipping yet another step in the process of acceptance, all because of a timetable. I needed to figure out what I skipped.

After dinner I picked up the phone to call my mom. What a great gift to have a mother who rode horses too.

"I must have missed a step, but what was it?" I asked her. No one-size-fits-all approach worked when it came to specific steps for training horses. They were individuals, and it required guesswork as to what each horse required.

"Hmmm. Nevada seemed fine accepting objects on her back from the ground." Mom paused and silence grew between us. I knew she replayed my description of the scene in her mind, pondering what had gone wrong. "Did you spend enough time desensitizing her while she walked around?"

"Maybe I fell short with that part." I sighed, knowing she was right. "I thought I had, but now that I think about it, I spent more time desensitizing her while she stood still."

"I know it's difficult, but don't let the competition put pressure on you. What happens if you aren't ready?"

"It's not something I want to think about. She'd probably return to the holding pen." Unsettled anxiety knotted my belly every time I considered the possibility of her not finding a loving home. I couldn't believe how much my confidence in training Nevada waned now. On another note, if we didn't show up in Kentucky, it tagged me as a horrible trainer for all to witness. "You're right, Mom. I'll work on desensitizing her more."

"Just do the best you can, Haley. That's all anyone can ask." My mom said the words with such tenderness it made me feel like that loved little girl who stayed home sick from school.

Except I was no longer that young, fearless girl. Despite my anxiety from the riding incident, I had to continue Nevada's training. No one else planned to help her. I had signed up for the enormous responsibility.

All the stars are lined up the way they are supposed to be. Good ole Paw Paw, once again showering his wisdom down upon me. He'd say I was exactly where I needed to be, even if the thought was painful.

The next morning an epiphany hit me like a metaphorical lightning bolt. I shook my head in disbelief as I leaned against the fence. "Nevada, I didn't realize I lost the main point of entering the contest." She ignored me, but that didn't stop me from confessing my guilt. "I wanted to prove my family wrong, that I can make a living as a horse trainer instead of a nurse. I was searching for my self-worth, but I forgot the main point of the makeover. The training is about you, not me. It's my job to gentle you enough so anyone can adopt you. It's about saving a wild horse. You deserve a good life and to have someone who loves you as much as I do."

A sharp pang in my chest reiterated how much I loved her. "Of course, I want you for myself, but I've been selfish."

Despite the bruises along my right arm and hip, I committed to staying true to my original intentions of putting her first.

Feeling energized, I dragged out a tarp, the rubber buoys attached to a rope, and several other devices to help desensitize Nevada. I removed her halter. We had developed enough communication between us now that it was time to trust my training skills. I still held onto my desire to have Nevada want to please me without using artificial aids, and we had come a long way since the lasso incident. My training methods might be more of a natural approach, and take twice as long, but Nevada's opinion mattered to me. Her agreement was paramount in developing a deep understanding between us, as well as building trust and friendship.

"I'll try with everything I have to win the contest, so I have more money to bid on you," I promised as she twisted her ear to listen to me. "I'll find a way to keep us together."

She tossed her head as though nodding, and tears choked me at the thought of losing her. All along I've known the stakes, I just no longer liked the game.

I started taking donations online and selling T-shirts with Nevada's brand—displayed on the left side of her neck where the hair had grown back white—printed on the front of each shirt to support our journey. I hadn't earned a lot so far, but every dollar helped.

The days passed by too fast. I doubled down on desensitizing methods by straddling the top rung of the fence, placing one leg over her, and retreating when she accepted my presence above her from both sides. I had to wonder how I had thought mounting her before was a good idea. Having climbed the fence, I leaned over and held onto the rope with the attached buoy and swung it over her back. She stood frozen as I bounced it against her side to imitate me moving while sitting on her, then I lowered it to the ground. She turned her head and watched with wide eyes, worried about the buoy, reiterating my misjudgment of sitting on her.

From the top rung, I placed my left leg over her, sitting on her for the briefest moment, only to slide off the other side. I repeated this process so often Nevada grew bored, which was the point of the exercise. She began trusting me enough to follow me on the ground over different obstacles. Developing leadership skills took patience and practice for both of us.

I tried not to think about how far we were behind, but it haunted me almost daily.

By day forty-five, I planned to sit on her again. I wanted to try riding her bareback with a bosal on her face, made of braided rawhide, allowing her to rest unless I gently used the reins, made of real hair.

After a lot of preparation, I asked her to step up to the mounting block. I rubbed her soft, warm hair. Somewhere along the line she had become my best friend.

"Take it easy on me, Nevada." She didn't answer but I understood her relaxed body and lowered neck to mean she agreed. With awareness, I took my time sliding onto her back, reading her body language to make sure she stayed relaxed. No worries. She remained still after I mounted. I'd done everything I thought of to prepare her. This had to work!

A flash of my childhood danced in front of me. I was on Wild Man once again, riding with the reins knotted on his withers, riding with my hands in the air and my feet dropped out of the stirrups. That sense of freedom resurfaced, and again, I realized my own liberation surfaced while in this ring, working with Nevada, with no one telling me what to do, or how to do it. This was the job of my dreams, although it barely felt like work, more of a passion than anything.

I sat on her for a long minute, relishing the precious moment of success, and then slid off as a reward. A couple of additional minutes ticked by before I mounted her again. Still no negative reaction, so I asked her to walk, a cue I had taught her during our preparation.

She took a tentative step forward, and then another step, and then another. I lightly pulled back on the reins to stop in place to test our communication, another activity we'd practiced from the ground. She halted rather suddenly, and I pitched forward. Thankfully, she didn't react. She stood perfectly still.

I rubbed her neck. "Good girl."

We walked again at my cue, and a surge of confidence circulated through me. I was riding her! She learned if she touched a cone when I asked, she received a treat that I kept in a small pouch hanging from my side with a strap.

Over the next several days, I worked her from the ground while she wore a western saddle. If there was one thing I learned, she required a lot of prep work before I got on her. My gut instinct said we weren't ready to try a saddle yet while riding. Today I introduced a different saddle to practice with, a heavy roping saddle. I held onto her with a long rope. After some repetition, she accepted the different saddle on her back without issue, proving I had desensitized her well, but when I reached for the girth underneath her belly, she darted to the side. The saddle fell off and landed with a thud on the ground. She scooted away from the pile of leather and toward me. I had to use my liberty whip to keep her from running me over.

Working with Nevada remained slower than slow. We took one beautiful step forward, riding bareback at a trot, and then for days after we'd slip backward from her fear-based reactions, requiring me to break down anything new into teeny, tiny increments. Every single stage she resisted, but once she accepted what she at first feared, then we didn't have to revisit the lesson. The next time I rode her bareback, I grinned as we jogged along a line of cones in the pen, and I experienced true joy.

I patted Nevada. "That, my friend, was one of the happiest rides of my life." Once we established consistency riding bareback, I'd be ready to take the big stride forward to sit in the saddle. My intuition warned me to make sure she was ready for such a task.

RUNNING OUT OF TIME

Ticktock sounded the clock as the days slipped away. With forty-five days left, my window of opportunity to train Nevada for Kentucky was running out.

I was learning that the makeover challenged me in more ways than one. Not only did I need to tap into more patience, somehow, I had to hold onto the belief that we'd make it to the competition. Realistically, I wasn't sure we would be ready.

I took extra days to make sure Nevada was consistently comfortable with me riding her bareback before I tried her with a saddle. I continued to sack her out with buoys, a tarp, and the large squishy ball.

We were supposed to compete in less than two months, which required riding her outside the safety of the small pen. The problem was, I had yet to sit on her with a saddle and no way would I ride her bareback outside the pen yet.

From a competitive standpoint, we didn't stand a chance. My friends cantered their horses in pastures, had fun riding over poles and other obstacles, and I could barely steer Nevada.

One day at a time; one step at a time.

I still held onto the dream of performing in Kentucky without a saddle and bridle, but there was one tiny little problem. If I lost her at the auction, the chance of someone else wanting to ride her only bareback was unlikely. I worked harder to desensitize her to various western saddles.

When I felt relatively certain that she had accepted a variety of saddles on her, cinched and all, I decided today was a perfect day to ride her with a saddle. My mom had arrived last night to keep tabs on us.

She hung out with me all morning, assisting me with the feeding routine of my animals. I enjoyed having her company. I didn't mind being alone most days, but today her presence meant more to me, so I didn't have to ride with Chris far off in the back field. He'd never hear me if something unfortunate happened. When it came time to work with Nevada, my mom leaned on the fence, mesmerized. After I placed the saddle on Nevada's back and prepared her to ride by moving her around and over objects from the ground, and then placing items on her back, Mom clapped.

"I'm impressed, Haley. You've made amazing progress with her."

"Thanks, I appreciate your support." What a relief to have her here. First times were always rough with Nevada, and it was hard to let go of the memories of that awful moment I sat on her bareback. Mom knew horses, and I valued her input. She also lent me a feeling of safety.

Standing on the mounting block, remembering all too well how our disastrous first ride went, I inhaled deep, calming breaths. A lot had changed since that day, and after a plethora of desensitizing strategies and riding bareback several times, Nevada had adopted a better mindset. I stuck my toe in the stirrup and lifted myself onto her. I despised having the awkward saddle between us and missed the warmth of her back as well as establishing a deep connection and feeling like one with her.

Without me giving her a cue, she stepped forward a few curt steps, tossed her neck downward, then took off like a bullet. *Oh, no!* I grabbed the horn of the saddle as she belted out a series of powerful bucks. Squeezing my thighs against the leather, attempting to stay glued to the seat, I bounced high and fast. My legs swung back and forth. When she jolted off the ground, her back feet kicked out with force, and she ducked her head low. I flew over her neck and hit the dirt hard, once again.

"Haley!" My mom ran to me. Dazed, I managed to sit up but did not try to stand.

As a pleaser, I felt I had to ease my mom's concern. I knew she was upset and worried about me, but I wanted to sit there without talking. My mood spiraled downward, along with my confidence.

She wrapped her arms around me, and I cried.

"Hang in there. You're both doing so well," she said, squeezing me. "Maybe there is something wrong with the saddle."

I knew she wanted to cheer me up, but there was nothing wrong with the saddle. Nevada had worn it many times before I sat on her.

"Haley, maybe it pinched her."

I shrugged. "Maybe."

Over the next week I tried three different saddles and finally found one that caused her not to buck when we moved, although I had only fallen from the saddle once.

I rode her with the saddle daily until she grew comfortable with the idea, but I paid dearly for the valuable time it cost. At this point, safety and the quality of my training meant more to me than a contest.

The next stage of instruction required me to lead her unmounted from the safety of the pen while holding a long line. I had no idea what to expect. We left the security of the confined area, and I left the gate open in case we needed to return in a hurry. Nevada glanced around the barnyard but didn't spook until Elvis ran out from the silo, gobbling his fool head off. She darted to the side, snorting at the turkey.

"Elvis, I have enough issues here. Go away," I commanded.

Instead, he gobbled incessantly. At least he didn't charge us, and I learned to ignore him as we strolled our way across the grass to the outdoor arena. I kept the lesson short and sweet. The next morning when I walked outside to feed Nevada and to complete my barn chores, I found Elvis in Nevada's pen.

"You better get out of there if you value your life," I advised.

He sassed me with a series of gobbles. To my surprise, instead of charging my horse as usual, Nevada approached him and sniffed his fan of feathers.

I watched in silence as she nuzzled him and nickered, mutual acceptance established between them.

"Unbelievable. I've seen it all." How many horses had a rescue turkey as a best friend?

After I had fed the animals and Elvis found his duck friend, I entered the pen. I walked Nevada through the usual training preparations and secured the saddle on her back. She almost seemed to enjoy leaving the pen. We worked in the sandy arena, and Chris sat down on the swing outside the fence to watch me. It wasn't often he took a day off, and I knew I didn't appreciate him near enough for everything he did for me. Nevada wasn't only teaching me new training skills but teaching me to appreciate life in general, especially my husband.

Another important lesson I wanted to learn was how to increase my knowledge about other training techniques. Throughout this competition, I'd seen a lot of different methods with the same end goal in mind, and although I still believed in my own training style, I started to realize other people's practices worked as well.

With the saddle in place, I trained Nevada from the ground with two long ropes, each running through a stirrup on both sides of her belly. We addressed steering, stopping, trotting. I still didn't use a bit in her mouth.

When she did well, I decided to mount her while Chris watched over us.

There were no bucks, although her body felt somewhat tense. What progress we were making.

During the following days, I rode her in the arena lightly. To advance our training to the next level, I invited our neighbor and her horse over so Nevada had a friend to trail behind, and to help relax her with the saddle. We learned to trot on command and worked on endurance at a sustained trot while following a horse, although steering remained an issue. We tackled walking and trotting over poles. I enjoyed every second, because I was finally riding my mustang.

Chris watched us from the swing again and clapped his approval. My mood soared. My self-confidence elevated a few notches, but in all truth, training a mustang had humbled me.

Nevada seemed happy and cooperative for the most part, because I hadn't introduced anything big and scary to her at this point. Once we reached the competition, I knew what faced us. Those horses performed astonishing tricks, and the pressure to perform became real. I researched how to teach Nevada to lie down on command by shuffling my feet in the arena sand and rewarded her with treats and loving pats when she figured out what I wanted.

"Good girl!" I found the trick exciting and impressive. I enjoyed playing with her as we ran free in the large, fenced-in arena. We swiveled in circles, and when I jogged off toward Chris, she followed me as if she enjoyed my company. My love for this horse soared to a new height.

Even though progress remained painfully slow, at least we were moving forward and making headway.

My neighbor visited once again, and for the first time ever, Nevada broke into a canter while I rode her. Unsure of how she might react to me on her back as she ran, I gripped the horn of the saddle, but she didn't buck. She almost seemed to appreciate the faster pace. We loped around the arena, leaving us both huffing to catch our breath.

While we had made huge progress from day one, at this rate we weren't progressing far and fast enough to compete. I needed to do something different if I wanted to make it to Kentucky, such as training Nevada to allow another person to touch her as well as handle and ride her. Then there was the actual competition, which included riding tests that required cantering in circles, crossing wooden planks as a makeshift bridge, and backing up through Lshaped poles. I had grown enough as a trainer to realize my own limitations. My friends were busy training their own mustangs, and I had no one to assist me.

I needed help now.

Dark thoughts slipped into the shadowy corners of my mind.

Come on, Haley. As Paw Paw used to say when I struggled with one of our horses, *You must do better than this. Be strong and do not give up, for your work will be rewarded.*

Keep going.

Perseverance. Determination. Belief.

The mustang makeover had prompted the biggest risk I had ever taken in my life. We had spent a lot of money we didn't have to pick Nevada up from Tennessee, to feed and care for her, to take time off work at the hospital, and to embark on the competition in Kentucky. There was also the added stress of me failing and Nevada returning to the holding pens.

My original intentions had been to save a wild mustang and to have a chance to prove myself as a real trainer. That wasn't so much the case now. I wanted my best horse friend to have a loving home, even if it wasn't ours.

I'd come this far, and I didn't plan to fail now.

But the proverbial time clock ticked away. We had less than a month left until the competition.

"Haley, there is a trainer I know named Deborah Gibson," my mom told me one day. "She won reserve champion in the 2012 Texas makeover. She also had an infamous freestyle performance without a bridle on her horse."

Kudos to Deborah Gibson! She had accomplished my dream, and I held the utmost respect for her.

The good news was she lived in North Carolina. The bad news? She lived four hours away and didn't normally teach lessons. I reached for the phone and called her.

"I'm in desperate need of help," I explained, being transparent. I mean, at this point I had nothing to lose. "I have a dominant mare who is bold. Everything must be her idea, and I can't convince her otherwise until she decides to accept what I'm asking. We take one step forward and twenty steps back."

"I feel for you," Deborah said in a soft, understanding tone. "How can I help?"

I paused. I wanted to avoid sounding too distraught but reasoned it was too late. "Would you be willing to help me if I trailered Nevada to you?" Nevada had only loaded in the trailer for practice a few times, but she never actually left our farm. I expected a lot by requiring her to travel four hours each way.

"As luck has it, I had plans this weekend but they were canceled. Would Saturday work for you?"

"Yes!" I needed to breathe and relax, so I didn't scare her off. Help was on the way. "Name the time, and we'll be there."

"How about ten? That gives us plenty of time to work together, except that's a long drive for you."

"Trust me, it's worth it." I sighed with relief. "We'll see you tomorrow."

Instead of texting Chris, I called him.

"Hey, honey." I knew he was in the back field but wanted to let him know I'd made plans. He needed to work this weekend anyway, and I had to make a split-second decision to accommodate Deborah's availability. What good luck.

"Wish I could go," he said after I explained the situation. "Can your mom join you?"

She lived a couple of hours in the opposite direction. "There's no way she can pull that off last minute."

I heard the tractor start up in the background. "I've gotta run, sweetheart, but have fun tomorrow. Love you."

I pocketed my phone and headed outside to feed the horses dinner. Stubby and Ringo helped me, starting with Gus the cow, then the horses and donkey. The chickens, duck, and lovely Elvis were next, then Nevada. I always saved her for last to teach her patience, plus I enjoyed watching her while she ate. It was more of a bonding moment for us, or at least for me.

I draped my arms across the metal plank of the fence and

hooked my boot on the lowest rung to watch her eat. "We have a road trip tomorrow, girl," I said to her as she licked the bottom of the rubber feed pail. When she finished, she stepped over to munch on a pile of hay. "We're going to leave bright and early in the morning, so you'll need to have good behavior trailering." I chose not to use Old Red, but to use a smaller trailer, a slant load we owned, simply because I felt safer driving to the coast with it alone, despite the increased difficulty loading her.

It had been at least two weeks since we had practiced. I had trailered horses by myself many times before and had taught Nevada to load herself while I stayed near the tailgate. This was our first trip off the property. I didn't expect a problem, but Nevada was unpredictable.

I cherished being able to devote effort to Nevada's training and didn't miss working at the hospital. Our patient caseload remained at a record low, and people scrambled for extra hours. Reluctantly, Chris accepted that I gave most of my hours away when possible, knowing full well I needed every spare moment with Nevada.

Twenty-four days before we left for Kentucky, and I had yet to ride her off the property, much less to trailer her to other facilities to practice.

We were still working on basic riding skills such as steering.

Was Kentucky even on the table? It was a close call.

The trip to Deborah's farm would help me figure out my next steps. I longed for a second opinion from a skilled trainer, one who had makeover experience and knew a realistic timeline for Kentucky. It was a lot to expect from one training session, but the best option I had.

I tossed and turned most of the night but woke up the following morning before my farmer husband, who usually arose well before dawn. I had just finished making scrambled eggs, toast, and bacon when I heard him get up to use the restroom.

When he walked into the kitchen, I set his plate on the bar. "Rise and shine."

He grinned as he sat down. "Be safe today. He shoved a large forkful of eggs into his mouth.

"We will." I rinsed my dish, stuck it into the dishwasher, and then kissed him goodbye, holding onto him a little longer than usual. I wished he were going with me, remembering the scary haul home from the mountains. I'd done this before. No big deal.

"Text me when you get there and before you pull out on your way back," he said with a sense of protectiveness I found attractive.

"Will do." I blew him a kiss and closed the door behind me to the carport. The dogs followed me throughout my morning routine instead of running off to the pond. Maybe it was too early to explore. The sweet scent of fresh hay floated through the early morning air, much warmer now than when I first started the makeover. The birds chirped in delightful song. There was something so wonderful about waking up on a farm. No traffic out front, no immediate neighbors, no noise other than nature.

While everyone happily munched on feed and hay, I pulled the trailer out from underneath the overhang of the training barn.

Stubby stood aside, and when I climbed from the truck, he barked at me.

"Sorry, sweets. You can't come along this time." He barked again. "Okay, you can go to Kentucky with us." Everyone brought dogs. Stubby was fine to join us, but Ringo always preferred to stay home. He didn't like entering our own house, so a hotel room was out, and he didn't walk on a leash all that well. Besides, he had never stayed in a crate. Ringo was a farm dog, and Stubby was my spoiled, precious sweetheart. He stopped barking and seemed satisfied with my answer.

Kentucky would be here before I knew it. My mom and a dear high school friend of hers planned to caravan with us through the mountains to the horse park, and I looked forward to having more support. My mother's knowledge was an asset, plus, I loved having her along for the journey.

Nevada finished eating the feed and searched for her hay,

which was piled in the trailer. She shook her head in protest. "Come on, girl." I gave a slight tug on the lead rope, but she planted her feet, refusing to budge.

"You have a treat in the trailer," I reasoned, trying to convince her with words she didn't understand. I tugged again. She protested at first but relented, thankfully, and decided to follow me. As we stepped closer to the trailer, she stopped in her tracks and raised her head to stare at the object parked in an unusual place.

"You've trailered before, and today is not the day to have an opinion." I wrapped the rope around her neck and pointed my finger. She decided she was okay and stepped inside.

See, all is going well.

Until that moment I hadn't realized the level of concern I held about her loading.

I placed my helmet on the passenger seat along with a day's worth of bottled water and a snack, then turned over the trusty old truck's engine. Everything so far was uneventful and what a blessing to have help. We were in safe hands.

Reminder to self, it was okay to ask for assistance. I didn't have to take on the weight of always doing everything myself. I had come a long way with allowing Chris, and now Deborah, to help me.

Today was a pivotal step in our journey. Nevada and I met each milestone one step at a time until we conquered our fears. Mind you, we had a lot of fears and more to overcome, but that was how training went. Personal growth, even. I felt confident, but on the way out of the driveway, a kick to metal rocked the truck.

"Point taken, Nevada," I called back to her in case she could hear me through the open window. I hoped she planned to settle down once we started down the road. She'd had plenty of hours on the trip from Lebanon, Tennessee to get used to the idea of trailering. And that drive had not been ideal. She had been wild and right out of the pen.

Preparation was important to me, but my difficulty with the

makeover was I needed more time. One hundred days was not enough to train her the way I wanted.

She eventually settled down, and the trailer stopped rocking. The four hours went fast enough, but I was glad to finally arrive. Deborah, a petite woman with stark black hair, greeted me with a baby on her hip as I stepped out of the truck.

"Thank you again. I appreciate your help," I said with sincerity.

"No worries. Glad you called, and I know how rough the last couple of weeks can be before the event." Deborah stood straight and wore a cowboy hat. Immediately, I liked her down-to-earth personality. The baby girl stole my heart, an unfamiliar niggle tugging at me.

"Does she tie to the trailer?"

I shook my head, trying not to laugh at the absurdity of Nevada tying anywhere. The only place I groomed and saddled her was in the round pen. It dawned on me I was even further behind than I thought. At least at the show she'd be in a stall when I performed those tasks. She had a stall attached to the round pen at home, and she did use it sometimes, coming and going at her own will, but in Kentucky she'd have to tolerate staying inside for long periods.

"Why don't I hold her while you get her ready?" She shifted the baby to her other hip.

I winced. "That's another issue too. Nevada doesn't let anyone else near her." There was the one time when Chris lassoed her, but she took no interest in him otherwise.

"You do know, if someone else wins her at the auction, they'll need to touch her."

I poked out my lower lip in frustration. "I know. It's been a point of stress for me. I'm wishing like anything that I win the bid for next to nothing. We don't have abundant funds, and I'm hoping no one takes an interest in her."

She nodded. "I understand the bond you feel and hope you win. Let's see how much we get done today. I'll be honest with you about my thoughts on where you both stand."

"Fair enough." My stomach knotted, and I had no idea what to expect. The first time off the farm was usually a big deal for most horses, and Nevada didn't handle first times well. "We've never ridden in an arena other than ours."

Bless her, she smiled with empathy. "Let's see how she does. Now is a good time to start. Feel free to use the round pen to saddle her up. I can carry the brushes."

Thank goodness for round pens! I unloaded Nevada easy enough, but when she realized we were somewhere new, she danced around in circles. She called out to no one in particular, and a horse off in the distance whinnied at her. I juggled the saddle in one arm and led Nevada with the other.

I held on to the lead rope while I brushed her in the corral, and it wasn't easy. I wished I trusted Nevada enough to let Deborah hold onto her, but I had to pick my battles, and she was holding a baby. There were too many things to tackle in one day.

I pulled the saddle off the fence and managed to tack her up, but it took longer than usual. When we finished, Deborah said, "Head on into the arena." She pointed to an open pipe gate, and I led Nevada toward it.

Deborah's husband joined us and lifted the baby out of her arms and into his. That soft little niggling of desire got me. Apparently, bonding with Nevada brought out my motherly side and planted a hint of yearning that began to stir inside me. She introduced me to her husband and he reminded me a lot of Chris.

When Nevada and I entered the arena, she held her head high, ears pointed, and stepped with more energy. Sure, she was nervous, but her rational behavior surprised me. I had experienced much worse situations than this. I took her reaction to mean she was learning to trust me.

We worked on several exercises from the ground to keep Nevada focused on what I asked of her. When she relaxed, I climbed into the saddle. We walked straight, in circles, and over poles on the ground. When she calmed more and listened to me well, I asked her to trot. Deborah taught me the overwhelming expectations of each class at the competition and how to prepare and navigate them. She gave me in-depth instruction until my brain became overloaded.

"Keep practicing these skills at home. She'll have to step into their trailer at the show. Another task is to demonstrate light grooming skills, preferably with the lead rope placed on the ground while you walk around her. You'll be the only one in the indoor arena, and it's huge. The acoustics are horrible and scary for a horse. I think it's a great idea to take her to the North Carolina fairgrounds in Raleigh for the upcoming horseshow."

"I was considering showing her there," I said, feeling nervous and excited at the same time.

"Good. You can acclimate her to an outdoor and an indoor arena with acoustics. The show will be smaller and a great first experience to help her get used to people milling about and the announcer on a loudspeaker."

Experiencing acoustics in an indoor ring for the first time usually caused issues, and Nevada didn't normally respond well to new demands. I tried not to overthink the situation for now.

Speechless by how much I still had left to address, I decided to accept my mustang friend Katie's offer to also ride at the equestrian college where she worked. It wasn't possible to visit too many different arenas, and the college had an indoor arena without a show happening.

"The stranger danger ... You have enough to work on, and no one else will be riding her at the show," Deborah explained. "Let's just hope you win her at auction. I'd focus on the other issues and leave the fear of strangers for last. You could always work on that at the Raleigh horseshow, but there will be so much going on there, I wouldn't worry about it. Scrape that off your plate."

Her words opened a floodgate of relief for me. If I didn't have to worry about her being handled by someone else, that would free me to focus on the skills we needed to even make it to the Kentucky competition. The program expected this of me, but if

I didn't feel she was ready, I knew I'd have a problem on my hands. She'd likely wind up returning to the holding pens, and Nevada would never get her forever home. In my mind, that wasn't an option.

When our lesson was over, I stepped away from Nevada and gave Deborah a big hug. "Thank you so much for everything. I didn't know how much I didn't know." We both laughed.

"You'll be fine. You have a couple of weeks left, and now you have a plan."

"I feel like this is the turning point in our training," I said, full of gratitude.

I led Nevada to the trailer and pointed, but she stared at me with a silent but unmistakable *no*. She turned away and tried to drag me toward the round pen, but I sunk my heels deep into the sandy dirt and yanked on the lead rope. Thankfully, she stopped, and I led her back to the trailer and pointed, but again she refused.

Deborah stood at a safe distance from us and watched. "Try walking her on the trailer. You'll have to do that at the event anyway."

I hadn't considered the trailering task in much detail for the competition. I shortened the lead rope and walked with confidence to the trailer, but Nevada stopped suddenly, jerking on the lead rope and refusing to move her feet. My cheeks blushed with heated embarrassment. I had skipped yet another important step, and now I grew apprehensive about the judged trailering obstacle at the makeover. Just what I needed, more stress.

It took two hours to convince Nevada to load.

She didn't do anything easily!

If we failed the trailering obstacle at the event, then we would likely lose the competition and the prize money Haley needed to adopt Nevada.

FOLLOW THE LEADER

The countdown began. We were set to leave for Kentucky in a mere fifteen days. I didn't feel ready, not yet.

Except for visiting Deborah, Nevada and I existed in the safety of our own protective bubble on our farm. We had a lot of work left, and my friends offered to help.

Today, we ventured outside our comfort zone to Henry Community College to meet Lisa and Katie.

Nevada and I practiced the problem-solving approaches Deborah had taught us that related to trailer loading. Our progress wasn't perfect, not that perfection was achievable or even ideal, but Nevada did step into the trailer after the third try. The trip to the college took about thirty minutes. What a wonderful opportunity to prove to her that not all trips were four to ten unbearable hours. I wanted to solidify this important lesson before the long drive through the winding mountains to Kentucky.

When we arrived at the college, I pulled onto a grassy section just outside an outdoor arena. It was larger than mine at home and offered a wonderful opportunity to ride with my friends and their mustangs. What a smart move to come here. My friends stood with their horses near the large indoor arena, waiting for me to unload Nevada. They were aware of Nevada's stranger danger and the difficulties we had faced to this point. What good friends to agree to help me.

Nevada hesitated to step off the trailer, reminding me of the first night we brought her home from Tennessee in the pouring rain, except this time I held a rope attached to her halter. "Come on, girl."

She tossed her head, not wanting to back out of the doorway. I realized that required trust but having confidence in me was at the crux of training a horse. Without trust we had nothing. She relented and stepped backward a few steps but then retreated. I waited until she was ready on her own terms, but I didn't miss the important, underlying message here. Life had its own pace, meant to be experienced with slow, deliberate appreciation, and wasn't meant to be rushed to the finish line. I breathed in, paused, and valued what time I had left with her.

After several minutes of waiting, Nevada surprised me by scrambling off the trailer. What a difference it made when it was her own idea as opposed to me asking her. Katie's horse, Bonnie, whinnied, and Nevada tossed her head high and pelted out a loud whinny in my ear.

Bonnie called out again. They held a conversation, and I was sure they knew each other.

Nevada darted in a circle around me. She didn't take her eyes off Bonnie, and with the power of a bulldozer, she dragged me toward Katie's horse. I was too stunned to correct her, and my heart squeezed at the touching scene unfolding in front of us.

"I've never seen anything like this," Katie said, smiling and clearly feeling her own set of emotions.

"One time I witnessed a foal returning to her mother a year later," Lisa said with feeling in her voice. "They recognized each other right away. Maybe Bonnie and Nevada lived on the range together."

"It's possible. Maybe they were friends." My throat choked up from raw affection. The touching scene wrenched my emotions, and once again I wondered about removing the mustangs from the range. Then an opposite thought took hold of me. They were alive, fed well, and loved.

"That would be amazing if they are related," Lisa said,

holding her mare, Magnolia, as she grazed nearby.

"Let's get ready to ride," Katie said, giving Bonnie a pat when the two horses lost interest in each other. "I'm eager to see how you're doing with Nevada."

"Me too. Let's start in the outdoor arena first," Lisa suggested, her horse standing still by her side. What a well-trained animal.

I was eager to ride in the indoor arena but wanted to tackle something familiar first and within my comfort zone, so it made sense to start in the outdoor ring. I wished I had practiced tying Nevada to the trailer at home this past week to make grooming easier, but it hadn't been the highest item on my list to check off. I made the best of trying to hold her while multitasking and now was a befitting time to practice the grooming obstacle for Kentucky.

I brushed Nevada near the trailer, usually grooming her in the round pen at home. She stood still as if she had done it many times before. Already we'd made progress today, and I was glad for the opportunity. When we met the others in the ring, I watched in awe as they rode and steered their horses with ease. Disappointed but facing reality, I tossed away my dream of riding in the competition without a saddle or bridle. The reality check was real. The amount of training that still faced us dazed me.

I had viewed several videos online where trainers performed stunning tricks during the championship class, such as having their horse bow or sit on a couch. Their amazing achievements played out with fun music playing overhead on the sound system.

My goal was simply to compete in Kentucky. Period.

My friends busied themselves by trotting, cantering, spinning in circles. I worked on the basics of steering Nevada at the walk and trot to keep her on a semi-straight line. She spooked at the jumps, having never seen the obstacles before.

Both Lisa and Katie were lightyears beyond where I stood with Nevada. Our lack of progress hurt but at least we were making headway. I faced a difficult moment where my ego and reality conflicted. Who did I think I was, wanting to prove myself as a professional trainer? *Ha*!

The makeover had done nothing but prove my inadequacies and deflate my self-esteem.

My friends' horses trotted over poles, where Nevada remained content to walk over them. They cantered around and performed sliding stops.

The real reason popped into my mind of why I entered the program to begin with. I wanted to save a wild mustang, so she found a loving, forever home. Who cared what people thought? Not that my friends judged me, but I needed to stop comparing myself to other people. Nevada and I were doing the best we could do, at the pace that worked for us.

I rode up to my friends, who stopped in the middle of the arena to chat. "Can I ask a favor?" When they glanced at me, smiling without judgment, I asked for their help with cantering.

Paw Paw used to say that teamwork was the way to succeed in life. Maybe he was right. I usually avoided asking for help, being an independent woman and all, but since joining the makeover I was changing my mind about reaching out for assistance. I first noticed the shift when I let Chris help me lasso Nevada, and then out of desperation I called Deborah for guidance. Maybe being vulnerable enough to allow people to help me proved beneficial, and even demonstrated growth on my own part. I wasn't the only one learning from the makeover experience. I glanced down at Nevada and patted her.

Lisa and Katie suggested we play follow the leader behind them.

"Try it by yourself now," Lisa encouraged.

I flashed them a thumbs up, and off we went. Nevada stepped into the canter without issue and made me proud. I grinned like I won the lottery and let her stop to rest while I patted her neck.

"Let's try again, longer," I said to Nevada.

We cantered alone next to the arena fence to help with steering. She tried to run to the other horses parked in the middle for comfort—the closer to them the better—but I was able to keep her near the fence where I wanted. We worked through the issue, and my worries lifted about being alone in the arena at the competition. That held its own set of challenges, though, but all we could do was our best.

I guessed I never got over being dumped after our first ride, and her reaction to new tasks. It was time to grab my anxiety by the horns and to stop allowing it to interfere with my training efforts. Enough already. Here we were, riding with friends. Enjoy.

Lisa and Magnolia practiced simple lead changes by adding a trot step to change direction. They made it look easy. Here I was working on simply directing my horse, but who cared? Today we had improved, and at least we were able to canter alone.

Lisa and Katie helped me work on sliding stops and simple lead changes, and even pivoting in circles. None of our moves were fancy or polished, but now that I realized more of what I needed to address, I planned to practice at home.

"I'd like to try something new," Katie said, eyeballing a leftover Christmas tree sprawled out on the ground in the center of the arena. I'd never thought to save one to use as an obstacle. "Lisa, can you hand that to me?"

The tree stretched to at least five feet in length.

Lisa grinned. "Are you kidding?"

"Not at all."

Lisa climbed off her horse and grabbed hold of the rope attached to the trunk of the pine tree. "What are you going to do with this?"

"Drag it behind my horse." Katie leaned forward in her saddle to reach for the limb.

My protective instincts kicked in. I couldn't imagine tackling such a stunt on Nevada, but what a great way to desensitize a horse. Nevada and I watched from the center of the ring while Lisa stood next to her horse.

Katie urged her horse to walk, but when Bonnie realized the tree followed her, she scooted forward and to the side. "Easy. You're fine." The horse scurried and snorted, but before long they walked with ease around the ring without issue.

"Unbelievable. See that, Nevada?" I asked as I sat on her. She continued to stare at the tree but didn't react. I wished I were around these adventurous women all the time so that Nevada and I could learn more.

"Let me try," Lisa said, climbing back onto her horse. Katie passed the rope attached to the tree to her. Magnolia stood still like a champ. Talk about trust. If I didn't know better, I'd think they'd performed this stunt many times before. Lisa urged her horse to walk forward. Magnolia had the smallest reaction, darting off to the side, then forward for the briefest burst, but then the horse's reaction diminished. They walked the arena like professionals.

"Your turn," Katie said to me.

I shook my head. I didn't think they realized what a rough time I had training this mare. "I value my life."

"We're right here. What better place to try than with us?" Lisa cued her horse toward me while dragging the blasted tree with her.

Nevada spun on her heels to stare at the scary object.

"Whoa, girl," I said, deciding to cowgirl up once again. Nevada relied on me for leadership, and I knew the pine tree wasn't a threat. My responsibility was to show her it wasn't terrifying, so I needed to stay relaxed. I inhaled a calming breath. At past makeovers, horses achieved far more adventurous stunts than this.

Lisa leaned forward in her saddle and handed me the rope.

Nevada shot forward, and then sideways while snorting at the tree. If she walked, it followed, so she pranced in place.

"You're okay," I said to reassure her. "A little ole tree won't hurt you." I asked her to stand quietly, and to my surprise, she listened. One step at a time, we inched forward. While her eyes remained wide, her breathing heavier than normal, I focused on inhaling my own calming breaths. Eventually, she lowered her neck and let out a long sigh. We walked around the arena dragging a Christmas tree like we owned the place.

I let go of the rope, and Katie rode over to me and smacked a high five on my hand. "Way to go! You're ready for the competition."

"Almost ready," I agreed. "I have two big quests left. We still need to ride in an indoor arena, and to tackle her stranger anxiety. She won't let anyone else touch her." Interesting how Bonnie's close proximity didn't seem to bother her, nor did Katie's as long as she sat atop Bonnie.

"At least you're the only one handling her at the show," Lisa said, parroting Deborah's words as she rode up alongside me. The three of us hung out in a group, filling me with a sense of deep, supportive friendship I'd never forget. I planned to stay in touch with these two wonderful women forever.

"Let's venture into the indoor arena and knock that off your list." Katie cued her horse to walk to the gate. We followed her lead.

I envied the fact she worked here and rode her horse with Lisa all the time. What great exposure, and what fun.

The indoor arena was a positive experience and for the most part, uneventful. I worked on the same skills I'd learned outside to give Nevada a chance to practice them in a different environment.

When we finished, we stood together to chat and laugh.

"Lisa and I are attending the horseshow in Raleigh next weekend. Want to join us?" Katie leaned forward in the saddle to swat a fly off Bonnie's neck. "It will give you an opportunity to ride in a new place, plus a low-key show experience."

"I planned on going anyway and would love to meet you there." Perfect, I didn't have to go it alone, and experiencing our first show with them sounded fun. I had also agreed to teach an informative demonstration on mustangs.

"It's a perfect place to let them get used to the acoustics of the arena and hearing an announcer over the loudspeaker without a lot of extra stress," Lisa said, taking her feet out of the stirrups to relax.

"And to grow comfortable with a small crowd," Katie added.

She sat slumped in her saddle, just hanging out. I loved her easy-going way.

"What do you think, Nevada? Want to go with friends?" I asked. She tossed her head up and down. "She says yes!" Nevada was likely shooing off a fly, but I found the interaction amusing. She had so much personality.

The three of us laughed. It felt good despite the tension of the makeover journey and the upcoming competition. I had spent a tremendous amount of time home alone, working with Nevada, and I missed hanging out with women.

At the end of the afternoon, Nevada loaded into the trailer with some hesitance, but at least it didn't take two hours as it had at Deborah's. She hadn't been the same loading since the four-hour ride back home, but I'd take any progress at this point. Showing gratitude proved, no matter how small, a helpful exercise to increase my positive mindset. That said, the trailer loading obstacle in Kentucky still loomed over us, but I'd deal with that later. Today we took another leap forward.

Once I returned home and settled down for the night, I checked social media. I received five different messages from people interested in bidding on Nevada. The threat of losing her was never more real. It seemed impossible to let her go, to see her walk away with someone else after the auction. The thought hurt so much I wanted to vomit. Chris and I needed to have an in-depth financial discussion to figure out how much money we had, if any, to allocate to my bid for Nevada. My worst fear was not being able to bid on her at all.

I answered the inquiries with unbiassed honesty, but dread filled me. To be fair to Chris, he had been upfront with me about the dangers of me falling in love with Nevada, and honestly, I thought I could handle keeping that boundary. I failed miserably because I loved her, and the possibility of losing her was unfathomable.

How devastating to feed my animals in the morning without seeing Nevada waiting for breakfast in the round pen. I loved those precious moments of leaning on the fence, watching her eat, connecting with her. Lately, she seemed to enjoy our routine too, and most days she walked over to me after she finished, so I could rub her face and love on her.

I had no idea how I had grown so attached, but I loved her with more intensity than I had experienced in all my years. I thought I felt that way about my other horses, Trigger, or Wild Man as I preferred to call him, and Junior, but not even close.

Nevada was my heart horse, a horse of a lifetime.

HORSIN' AROUND

I began to play with Nevada more. Our love for each other grew daily, and I tried not to think about the impending auction. We had one more event at the Raleigh fairground scheduled this upcoming weekend, but other than that, I planned to spend our remaining days together having fun. Even riding her in our outdoor arena became a happy ritual.

Today, I had a photographer friend visit us to take video and snapshots of Nevada and me, in case I never saw her again after our last thirteen days left together. I brushed Nevada until she shined and then chose one of the few cute tops I owned for the photo shoot. I wore my best pair of jeans, western boots, and the cowboy hat Chris bought me in Tennessee. I kept my hair long instead of pulling it back off my face in the usual ponytail. I wanted casual, carefree photos.

I'd never forget this day. At least I would have pictures to remember her and our precious journey together.

I choked down my complicated emotions and found my smile.

With the photographer snapping away, I took off running through the arena, my hair blowing behind me. I glanced back at Nevada as she followed. We played, ran in circles, and I laughed. What a change from working hard almost endlessly. It was as though she knew today was special too. I gave her the command to lie down and lifted her face to plant a tender kiss on the tip of her soft nose. She even closed her eyes when my lips met her muzzle. I heard the camera click, thrilled the photographer caught the precious moment of one loving cowgirl and one trusting horse.

I wanted ordinary pictures of everyday life, so I climbed onto her bareback, with only a bosal made of rawhide for the nosepiece and a simple headstall as a bridle, no bit. The black and white striped, roped reins made from horsehair added a striking point of interest. I bent down to hug her neck and the photographer snapped a photo. We posed in front of the picturesque pond with peaceful reflections of the tall green trees shimmering on its surface. Then we moved in front of a small marsh field, using a blanket of forest green as a rich backdrop. I laughed, enjoying every moment of every second. Nevada perked her ears for the camera like a natural model, as though never wild, and let me pose.

I slid off her and tossed a thick square pad on her back, then positioned the western saddle and remembered the first time I tried to ride her as well as when she bucked me off from the saddle. What a long way we'd traveled.

"I won't give up on you, girl," I whispered, my motto throughout the makeover. She turned her head toward me, and our eyes met for a long, emotional moment. I tried not to cry. The last thing I wanted was somber photographs to remember her by.

I climbed back onto her, posed for the lens, and then rode her with heart. Guess I was feeling nostalgic but cantering across the arena reminded me of the freedom I had with Trigger, Wild Man as I liked to call him, when I was a little girl. It was so tempting to drop my reins, to stretch out my arms as I had done back then, but I didn't dare. I wiped my freestyle dreams out of my mind as fast as they entered. They wouldn't manifest in Kentucky, but maybe someday when we were at a different place in our lives. Wanting to compete in the makeover became my new desire.

The horse show at the fairgrounds arrived far too fast, signifying the end of our journey and Kentucky right around the corner. We still needed to address the stranger danger if the opportunity presented over the weekend, but the makeover encroached on us like a stalking animal waiting to pounce.

When Chris and I pulled through the gate to enter the horse complex in Raleigh, I drew in a long, jagged breath.

"You okay?" Chris asked.

I nodded and took a moment of silence before I answered. "This is our last endeavor before we head to the makeover."

He exhaled a soft whistle. "That's big." He placed his hand on my knee and I absorbed his loving touch. We drove to a grassy area near one of the several barns. "You've got this, Haley."

I smiled in appreciation.

Nevada unloaded off the trailer with her head held high. She glanced around, planting her feet in the grass until she felt comfortable enough with the new environment. When she relaxed, I led her down the aisleway to a stall marked Haley Horsemanship. I had a proud moment when I saw my business name on the stall. I needed to own my success if I wanted to establish a training barn.

I tossed two flakes of hay in the back corner of her stall and filled up water buckets while Chris unloaded my supplies out of the trailer. I had spent several hours preparing and memorizing what to say and do for our demo, but my main goal of the show was to help Nevada grow accustomed to people moving around. I also needed to acquaint her with the acoustics in the arena, and to perhaps have someone besides me touch her. Acclimatizing her to people, even in the simplest form, remained my sole responsibility. As far as others riding her? Forget it.

After we unpacked and were settled, I walked Nevada around the grounds to let her experience the busy environment. She raised her head to watch horses and people come and go from all different directions. We rode outside in the open arena, and then the covered ring, before we ventured indoor on foot.

One other woman led her curious mare from the ground like me. When the staff tested the loudspeaker, Nevada jumped in place, but she calmed down more quickly than I expected.

By the next day, she had fully adapted to the environment. I glanced at my watch. "Are you ready to head toward the covered arena for the workshop?" I asked Chris. Gratitude filled me that he supported my mission to help Nevada.

"Absolutely," he said with that sexy, lopsided grin I loved. We walked through the showgrounds together, and then parted ways when I entered the arena. He headed toward the bleachers to watch us, and I led Nevada toward the waiting crowd. They were here to watch, to listen, and to learn about wild mustangs and natural horsemanship. People *wanted* to hear what I had to say.

We passed the empty judges' stand off to the side, which Nevada eyed slightly, and I marveled at how levelheaded she was behaving. I was proud at how far she had come. We sauntered to the far corner where people waited with patience to listen to my talk. It was standing room only, as people stood near the railing and others sat on the small group of bleachers. My mom sat on the left side of the bleachers, and my dad watched from the right. Divorce was so awkward.

My nerves twitched. I didn't like being the center of attention, but it was the next logical step in the progression of Nevada's training and mine. This was what I wanted. A man handed me a headset with a microphone that looped around my ear and allowed me to free my hands.

I closed my eyes for a moment. *Oh, please let me have the words to say.* A wave of relief filled me.

Here we go. Inhale, exhale, speak.

Nevada remained quiet, as if she had done this several times before. All our preparation had paid off, but Kentucky would be more intense, with more spectators, more competition. This event presented as the perfect place to prepare.

Nevada's summer coat shined, revealing her underlying gorgeous buckskin color with a plethora of dapples. Her black legs and mane resembled the color of coal. I ran my hand over the brand on her neck, proud to present Nevada to strangers.

The crowd hung on my words, Nevada a natural star. To think this horse had once been wild in the desert, and here she stood, showing off all her beauty for the crowd. I explained the history behind the mustangs, the BLM—Bureau of Land Management—helicopter gathers, and training in general. We demonstrated walking over a tarp, performing the Spanish walk as she extended her legs with exaggerated movement. She lay down on command and made me proud.

When we finished, people applauded. Nevada jumped in place, having never heard such a noise before, but she settled right down. Pleased with her, I returned her to the stall. I didn't allow anyone to touch or pet her yet. I then headed to the indoor arena to meet with curious people who had more questions about mustangs. My passion showed as I talked about Nevada. When they asked about Kentucky, I explained my strong desire to win the auction to keep her. I had plenty of people on our side who wanted to see me keep her and to follow our story on social media.

When I returned to Nevada, I led her out of the stall. A well-known trainer named Naomi approached us, apparently having watched the portion of our workshop when I mentioned Nevada's stranger danger.

"I can help with that," Naomi said. She reached forward and grabbed hold of the long rope, pulling it from my hands.

As a pleaser by nature, I let her take control of Nevada, despite my hesitance. If anything, I reasoned that Nevada had an opportunity to experience someone else, a brave and established woman. I tried to warn her about Nevada's history, but she ignored me and led her to a gravel area. People began to gather around to watch.

Nevada pinned her ears and closed the gap between them.

Naomi swung the lead rope in the air. "Don't let her disrespect you like that. This is how you handle the situation." She began to slap Nevada in the face with the rope.

Nevada raised her head to avoid the slaps but didn't back up and relinquish her dominance.

The woman continued as I stood there in horror, too frozen to respond. Out of the corner of my eye, I saw a man walk into my peripheral vision. My dad.

What horror. Not only was this woman belittling me in front of a small crowd after I finished teaching a workshop on training, but my dad witnessed the humiliation. Now my family would never believe I held the qualifications to be an accomplished trainer.

Regardless of what anyone thought, I had to save my horse. Pushing my embarrassment aside, I hurried toward Naomi and grabbed hold of Nevada's rope. "I have her from here," I said, not giving her a choice as I yanked the rope from her hands. "Thanks." Why did I feel the need to thank her? This was where my people pleasing stopped, if for no other reason than to help Nevada.

The woman shrugged and off she went with her following.

I rubbed Nevada's face. "I'm so sorry, girl!" What a horrible first experience for her. Like Deborah said, no one else had to work with Nevada except me. She deserved better, but in my heart, I knew the horse needed to trust other people. Even if I won her at the auction, at some point she had to increase her tolerance of others handling her. What if something happened to me, but I was the only person she allowed to touch her? If I didn't correct this in a positive way, my good intentions were a disservice.

Katie approached us. "Are you entering the trail class? It's up next."

"Yes, and thanks!" I hurried back to the barn, with my dad following us while trying to make small chat. Thank goodness he didn't mention Naomi and that fiasco. I tried to respond to him accordingly, appreciating that he took the time to attend the event to support me, but I was in a hurry to saddle up Nevada and to have Chris attach my competition number. On the trek to the outdoor arena, my mother joined us but kept a healthy distance from Nevada.

"I enjoyed watching your mustang demonstration."

I wanted to stop to give her a hug but kept walking, keeping our space.

"Me too," my dad added.

"Thanks, and I'm glad you're both here." I despised that he

had seen Naomi belittling me but there wasn't a thing I could do to change the circumstance.

When we reached the ring, I tried to mount Nevada, but she must have picked up on my jittery nerves because she moved around in a circle.

"Whoa, Nevada." No one could help me, so I had to accomplish this alone.

After another circle around me she planted her feet, and I pulled myself up into the saddle. We warmed up among the other horses in a smaller ring off to the side, still wet from the early morning rain. Riding with Lisa and Katie at the community college helped Nevada tolerate the light chaos now. We trotted and lightly cantered before walking to a spot near the gate to wait for our turn to compete. Katie sat atop her horse, having just shown in the class, but offering her support to me.

My father stood too close to Nevada for comfort. "Dad, she doesn't like other people. It's dangerous."

He glanced up at me. "She's fine."

Nevada pinned her ears. I gave her credit that she didn't attack him. His proximity helped increase her tolerance for people.

The gate attendant waved me on deck, and I cued Nevada to step closer but to maintain a healthy and safe distance from other horses. I watched the competitor in front of me as I fought off my rising nerves.

I patted Nevada's neck. "You've got this, girl. Just go in there like you've done this a million times." She flicked her ear back to listen to my words. "We've tackled all these obstacles before." Except for the small jump boxes filled with fake red flowers, the rest of the obstacles were familiar.

It was our turn. We entered the arena, the world blurring around us as I focused on the first task. She balked at the tarp lying on the ground, shouldered by two flower boxes, but with encouragement my brave girl stepped onto the plastic.

We moved on to the flower jump, but when she realized I wanted her to trot over it, she skidded to a halt and slid in the wet footing. She lowered her head to stare at the obstacle, swished her tail, but stepped over it with a stumble. I laughed, so proud of her.

She locked her gaze on the wooden platform, tried to maneuver around the ground pole in front as avoidance, but I squeezed her. Nevada skirted sideways over the pole and stepped onto the makeshift bridge and stopped in the middle of it as I asked.

When we finished our class and left the arena, I patted her sleek neck with enthusiasm. "Good girl! You did it!"

My mom grinned. "You've come a long way with her."

I practically glowed, soaking up her love and encouragement. "Thanks, Mom."

Chris joined us. "Way to go, girls. So proud of you." He kept his space, so I received his good wishes from a safe distance.

"Good job," Lisa said, having joined Katie and her horse near the arena gate. "I believe you are ready for Kentucky."

"Is that what comes next?" my dad asked, his arms crossed. Thankfully, he followed the other's cues to keep back.

"Yes, we travel to Kentucky in a little over a week." I could hardly believe it. The journey with Nevada, from day one until today, seemed so slow, almost endless, but now our time together swept by at a rapid pace.

"Want to caravan through the mountains?" Lisa asked, and I valued her planning skills.

"Sounds great, but my mom and her friend, Joe, are following us too. We'll meet them in Greensboro." I glanced at my mom for confirmation, and she nodded. "We want to drive at night. Less traffic and we can take turns sleeping."

"We planned to drive then, too," Lisa said. "Katie and I are traveling together. Want to meet at the last rest stop in North Carolina before we enter the Virginia mountains?"

We agreed on a time that worked for all of us and decided to text when we left home.

One of many takeaways from the makeover was how it brought people together, all with the goal to help our mustangs succeed in the new world. Then, of course, there was the unbreakable bond developed between horse and trainer.

Lisa and Katie followed us back to the barn, and Katie returned her horse to the stall. Before I unsaddled Nevada, Lisa offered to help.

"Let me. I'd be happy to assist with her stranger danger before the makeover." At my sideways glance, she insisted. "I'm a horse person and familiar with mustangs. I have her best interest in mind," she reasoned. "Better me than someone else."

I sucked my lower lip into my mouth. "I don't know. She's never had anyone else handle her." I didn't mention the debacle earlier. The thought scared me, but she made a good point. The possibility remained that someone at the makeover would try to touch or pet Nevada.

"I'll be careful."

I nodded and backed up as Lisa approached. She rubbed Nevada on the neck, letting her sniff Lisa's outstretched hand. Brave soul.

She took time getting to know Nevada and eventually loosened the cinch and removed the saddle with caution and handed it to me. As a reward, Lisa rubbed Nevada's belly. Without warning, not even a snort, Nevada lifted her back foot, and cow kicked Lisa. I heard an awful thud and a screech.

I gasped but Lisa remained calm as she bent over. She still held onto Nevada's lead rope but kept a safe distance away with a grimace on her face.

"Are you alright?" I handed off the saddle to Chris, who stood back with my family. The dazed look on my dad's face said it all as he stepped backward. I don't believe he had realized how difficult the journey had been with Nevada.

I hurried to close the gap between Lisa and me.

"I'm fine," she claimed, but her face paled. "It wasn't Nevada's fault. I surprised her."

"Let's get you checked out."

Lisa shook her head as she rubbed her right thigh. "I'm fine.

It just hurts a bit. If I'm not better by tomorrow, I'll call my doctor."

"Promise? We're leaving for Kentucky in just over a week."

She nodded, her pained expression causing me more concern. "I won't do anything to mess up the makeover."

I led Nevada into the stall before anyone else got hurt but had difficulty accepting the reality of Nevada kicking Lisa. I mean, it didn't really surprise me, as she hadn't accepted other people touching her, but still. *Lisa?* She was a professional.

"Why don't you sit down and prop up your leg. I'll get some ice," I said, the nurse in me taking over.

Lisa shook her head. "I'm okay. I have too much to do." Her face remained contorted, and she limped off. She was one tough woman!

Later that night, once we were home with Nevada safe in her pen, Lisa sent me a photo of the hoof-sized purple bruise on her thigh above her right knee. I covered my mouth and gulped.

"What's wrong?" Chris asked, taking a mouthful of his hamburger.

"Look at this!" I passed him my phone, sitting down next to him without grabbing my plate of food off the counter by the stove. I wished I had waited until after I had eaten dinner to look at the photo.

Chris whistled. "That's quite a bruise."

I crossed my fingers for Nevada to behave at the makeover. Looking at the photo made me realize it would take another miracle to pull off the competition, and I was already in deficit. I hoped there wasn't a scorecard being kept somewhere.

"Good thing we don't leave for Kentucky for ten days, or she might not compete. I can't believe Nevada did that to her."

"Believe me, I know without doubt what that horse is capable of. I've lassoed her before. Remember?"

"I'll never forget," I said, standing up to retrieve my plate and glass of water. "It's my responsibility to make sure she doesn't hurt anyone else. I need to win her back at the auction."

Chris frowned. "We only have so much money to bid, and it's not much. What will happen if someone else adopts her?"

We still needed to have the financial discussion I had been avoiding.

"I don't know." But I did know, and the outcome promised disaster.

BLUEGRASS CONUNDRUM

The day had finally arrived, the pivotal moment I had been both dreading and working so hard toward. *Kentucky.*

Mixed emotions clogged my throat, causing me to remain silent while I dealt with a strange combination of sorrow and excitement. To add to my trepidation, no stars twinkled in the dark sky overhead, promising rain for another road trip cross country.

I shoved my overstuffed suitcase into the backseat of the truck, doubting it possible for one more item to fit inside the vehicle. I placed my saddle—yes, I planned to compete with a saddle—along with a bucket of brushes into the small tack room of my two-horse, slant-load trailer.

With a flashlight, Chris spot-checked the truck and trailer one last time, especially the tires.

Nevada took several tries to load in the trailer but, thankfully, she didn't put up a huge fuss.

"Kentucky, here we come," I said to Chris as Stubby jumped onto the front seat. Our generous neighbor who had horses offered to feed our farm animals. We were ready to go!

I planned to sleep once we met up with my mom and her friend who wanted to follow us on our wagon train. For now, I was energetic, vacillating between nerves and excitement. Sometimes, it was difficult to tell which was which. I couldn't believe we were about to embark on our trip.

I tried not to imagine the return trip home, not knowing if my trailer would be filled with the lovely presence of my horse, or dark and empty.

"Here comes the rain." Chris turned on the wipers.

"That seems to be our travel theme lately." I tried not to think of the torrential rain in the mountains when we picked up Nevada, tried not to think of the wheel incident.

We made it to Mom's house in record time, thanks to the desolate roads. Oh, the beauty of driving at night. We turned off the highway onto the main road when my cell phone rang.

"Mom, we're almost there."

"We have a little problem. Joe is sick and can't come with us, so that means I need to ride with you. I don't want to drive all the way to Kentucky by myself."

I glanced at Chris, who shrugged. I had the phone on speaker as usual to include him in my conversations when we traveled.

Stubby slept on my lap because there was no room in the backseat, so I had no idea where to put my mom. "We're pulling in front of your place now," I said, disconnecting the call. "How are we going to do this?" I asked Chris, overwhelmed by this new change of plans.

"We'll figure out something." He shoved the gearshift into park. "I might be able to move some heavy items out of the trailer's dressing room and into the back of the truck. Things that won't matter if they get wet. We can shift some of the items from the backseat to the dressing room."

My mom locked the door behind her, an oversized suitcase in tow. Her grin shot a pang of guilt through me, and I knew without doubt I wanted her with us in Kentucky.

Chris rearranged the tack room, restacking the hay and then placing a bag of feed along with the pitchfork and other stall items in the bed of the truck. I dragged out my suitcase and Chris stowed it along with my mother's in the trailer. Thankfully, we made room enough for her to squeeze into the backseat with the plethora of items that remained.

We journeyed forward on our adventure. I had yet to check

my emails, so as we rolled down the highway, I pulled the app up on my phone. I sighed when I saw one from the makeover.

"What's wrong?" my perceptive mother asked.

"They're going to stamp a hip number on Nevada. What if she kicks them like she did Lisa?" Fear circled me like a hawk waiting to swoop down and snatch me into his talons. I didn't want anyone else to get hurt.

"Not good," Mom said, sitting up straighter.

I wanted to curl up in a ball, my emotions all over the place. "We've come too far to fail now. And we need to meet at the administrative tent at eight a.m. to stamp her."

Chris glanced at the time. "It'll be close, but we'll make it," he said with his usual calm demeanor. I appreciated and loved his gentle, logical nature.

We met Lisa and Katie at the last rest stop in North Carolina, and hugs abounded. I was blessed with horse friends and was glad to know we were in this together. We had come so far but still had a large hoop to jump through with the competition and auction facing us. Katie and I wanted to keep our horses, and Lisa planned to use her portion of the bid to help repay part of the cost of the makeover.

"How is your thigh?" I asked Lisa.

"Good as new," she said, lifting her leg and making a show of flexing and straightening it.

"You're tough." Lisa's ability to bounce back unscathed amazed me.

"Nah, it wasn't too bad," she said, brushing off the compliment. "What will you do about the hip number? I can speak from experience that Nevada isn't going to like that."

"No idea." My gut twisted into a large, tight knot.

The rainy drive through the mountains proved dark and curvy. Like our trip to Lebanon, Tennessee, I didn't sleep in the truck as I had planned. I worried about Nevada's behavior with the stamp, the show in general, the increased bidder interest on the website. The auction haunted me. Chris and I hadn't discussed the allotted bid amount in depth yet, so I planned to have that discussion soon.

I swear the dark ride through the hilly mountains symbolized the auction, the dreaded likelihood of me losing Nevada, and feeling as though I was preparing to enter a dark, scary cave without a flashlight. There was no turning back.

To distract myself from my awful thoughts, I watched motivational videos on my phone, turned to long, pleading prayers, and exchanged texts with Katie while Lisa took her turn driving their trailer. Nothing really worked to alleviate my excitement mixed with stress.

The rain continued to beat down, the wipers swiping fast. I watched the time, even though I had no control of the drive or weather. I closed my eyes and tried to calm my nerves. *Breathe in slow, breathe out slower.*

I must have drifted off at some point because when I woke up, I saw the sign in the headlights. *Welcome to Kentucky, Unbridled Spirit.*

I loved the phrase, as it described the makeover and my initial goal of competing Nevada without a bridle.

Chris and I switched turns driving so he could catch a few winks of sleep. We couldn't check into our hotel room until late afternoon, and I knew he was exhausted. I learned from the mustang experience how much he meant to me, how generous he was with his time and support, and I appreciated him more than ever. I also realized I needed to show my gratitude for him more.

The sun rose from behind the mountains. It filled the truck with a golden light and rejuvenated my energy. There was something special about the beginning of a sunny day in the country. The horse park was thirty minutes away, and each mile closer elevated my excitement. Chris and my mother stirred from their slumber. Even Stubby let out a long yawn and stretched out between Chris and me.

When we drove through the gate of the horse park, I pulled into the parking lot near the delegated barn, one of many on the showgrounds. The same newer rigs stared at me in the parking lot. Once again, I felt like the new girl in school with a rinky-dink trailer.

Funny how I was so full of myself back then. Sure, Nevada had intimidated me for a large chunk of the training process and my ego took multiple hits, but the program had taught me a lot. I'd had big plans for Nevada, such as our possible future together, but I was no longer the same woman. Being plummeted to the ground more than once changed a person.

"Haley, you got this," Chris said, apparently remembering my first reaction to the nicer rigs in Tennessee.

I turned to him and thanked him with a nod, no words necessary.

Being in Kentucky was darn near a miracle.

I pulled up near a grassy area and announced my plans to my sleepy crew. "I'm going to unload Nevada and take her for the hip stamp before I'm late. We can unpack the trailer when I'm finished."

Chris yawned. "Okay, I'll come with you."

"Me, too," my mom said, shuffling around the tight space in the back.

They climbed from the truck, my mom holding Stubby on a leash, while I unlatched the trailer door. Nevada stood near the front corner, her neck hanging low as if we awoke her. A sleepy Nevada could be a benefit or detriment, depending on if she woke up refreshed, tired, or irritable.

I didn't have time to gauge her mood. I unloaded her and headed straight toward the sign marking the hip-stamp area. There was one horse waiting. I kept my distance, wishing for the staff member's safety.

It was next to impossible not to notice Janice Johnson's decorated stall. A life-sized cardboard photo stood at the opening of the aisle, along with a hanging banner to advertise her training barn. From my research, I knew this fabulous trainer well. Janice had won a previous makeover, and I had the utmost respect for her.

Everything about her screamed polished, professional, and competent. My thoughts hung on the last word.

The horse in front of me stood like a champ when the familiar staff member, the one who had asked for the halter in Lebanon, stamped her hip. The horse didn't even flinch, but the stamp was farther back on the hip than I expected, a real concern. I imagined Nevada kicking the man across the aisle.

A young guy, an assistant and the one who had called Nevada a bruiser in Tennessee, raised his eyebrows and grinned at me. Yes, it was a surprise that we had made it to Kentucky.

Janice approached with her mustang and stood behind me. I fought the urge to shrink and battled intimidation. Her horse behaved well, she smiled, and even though I liked her instantly, I struggled not to feel inferior, as if I didn't belong here. Talk about having imposter syndrome. If Nevada didn't behave while having her hip stamped, I'd be mortified.

The man nodded at me, and we approached. I thought I better warn him, and perhaps he'd let me stamp her. "Sir, she's been a difficult horse from the get-go. She isn't used to other people handling her, so is it possible I can apply the stamp?"

He frowned. "If she doesn't let me stamp her, then we have a problem."

We had come too far in Nevada's training to turn back now. After all the blood, sweat, bruises, and tears involved, I'd hate to believe all this was a waste. I tried not to think about the copious amounts of money we'd spent to this point, what with time off work and dollars exhausted.

Nevada seemed tired from the long drive and stood still for me while keeping her gaze trained on the man. He approached and, thankfully, she didn't react. It became obvious he knew horses as he ran a confident hand along her neck toward her rump. He remained close, so if she did blast out a kick, it wouldn't cause much harm to him. He kept one hand on her, touched her rump with the stamp, and although she raised her head and widened her eyes, through a miraculous twist of fate the task was over. He stepped toward her head and dismissed us with a curt nod.

I patted Nevada. "Good girl!" Her behavior gave me hope for the competition.

The photographer snapped a picture for social media, likely to entice more bidders for the auction. Here we were, in Kentucky. This was where we discovered our destiny.

The young assistant flashed a grin, pulled off his cowboy hat, and saluted me.

"She was a bruiser, but we are here." I smiled with relief.

I joined Chris and my mom, who waited in front of Nevada's stall across the passageway from Janice's horse. Who knew, maybe I'd learn something from her. A better mindset than I had when I first joined the makeover.

I put Nevada in the stall and then went to unload the trailer with my family's help. We left poor Stubby behind, tied with his leash to a pole. When we finished setting up the tack stall where we stored the hay, grooming supplies, and my saddle, I led Nevada around the showgrounds to familiarize her with the new environment. Later that afternoon we checked into our hotel room to catch a long, wonderful nap.

The following day buzzed with activity and people riding their horses. Competitors crowded both arenas, the attached indoor warm-up ring, and the huge stadium. I stood at the gate to watch and marveled at the stadium's size, imagining people packed in the stands. Suddenly, I was happy I had brought Nevada to the smaller show in Raleigh. By the time we made it to ride in the practice area, the participant traffic had thinned.

Katie, Lisa, and I worked through our paces, working on our sliding stops, turns, and backing up. Nevada behaved well enough but seemed concerned about the other horses. Maybe her nerves mirrored my own. Once again, I realized how far we were behind but was grateful to have made it to Kentucky.

Amazing how significant events changed a person's perspective. I thought we'd be riding without a bridle and saddle in an arena filled with observers, and now I appreciated that she even allowed me to sit on her.

After we finished, Chris and I sat in a slice of shade on the grassy hill behind the arena while Nevada grazed and Stubby rested near me.

"You nervous?" he asked, reading my mind.

I leaned back on my elbows and nodded. "Nevada and I are at a basic level compared to others." I admired her sleek, beautiful dapples as she ate near me.

Chris shrugged his right shoulder and stared at me with those kind eyes of his. "Wasn't one of your goals to make it to the competition?"

"Absolutely. That's simplifying it, but yes. I also have the pressure of having my family, coworkers, and friends watching the live stream of the competition online. And you and Mom traveled all this way. No stress." Here I was, again concerned with what people thought of me. I was also competitive.

"No stress at all, Haley." His lighthearted spirit poked a hole through my armor of tension. "At least they're watching. They care."

I picked a clover out of the grass and chewed on the stem. "I suppose you're right."

Stubby sensed my distress and licked my chin. I pulled my dog into a hug and absorbed his love. We had driven this far, and it was up to me to do my best, to demonstrate what a rock star Nevada had become over the last three months.

When we returned to Nevada's stall, people milled around in the aisle with curiosity as they studied each mustang.

"They are bidders," I said in almost a whisper to Chris. "They're trying to decipher which horses to bid on at the auction." I fought off rising panic and an overwhelming desire to steer Nevada back to the grass, but I couldn't avoid them forever.

A family of four caught a glimpse of Nevada. Their two kids ran toward us, but I stopped them short, not wanting Nevada to kick anyone. They caught the hint and stepped back, but a man and his son approached with determination. I sneezed at his strong cologne and fought the urge to ignore him by walking straight into Nevada's stall.

"Beautiful horse," he said, analyzing her. "She's big enough to pull a carriage in downtown Charleston."

I glared at the man. Losing my horse wasn't ideal, especially to someone who wanted Nevada to haul tourists down streets all day long.

I whipped around to face Chris and almost plowed into him. I tried to keep my voice low so the man and his son wouldn't hear my words. "We need to have our money discussion tonight."

BIDDER INTEREST

The last activity of the day required trainers to meet in the arena with our horses for a question-and-answer session for interested bidders. Feeling aloof, I didn't say much. I sat on Nevada and hung out with Lisa and Katie.

People scattered along the stands, and Lisa answered a handful of general questions, but then again, she wanted someone to adopt Magnolia. Katie received a couple of questions, and I did too. My belly knotted until we left the arena. Thankfully, the memorable man and boy didn't follow me to the stall, but I knew he wanted to bid on Nevada.

After dinner, Chris and I returned to the hotel room to shower, rest, and have our money conversation to determine an agreed amount for my bid. The subject made my insides twist like a pretzel.

"I realize money is tight, but I can't imagine returning home without her, Chris." I pleaded my case to start the discussion, vying for an undetermined amount to win Nevada, despite our agreement before I signed up for the program.

"I knew you'd fall in love with her, sweetheart." Chris's voice remained kind but stern. He wanted to protect our money and to manage the finances of the farm, which was fair enough. "I understand your bond with her, but we can't spend what's allocated for other expenses. Unfortunately, life doesn't work that way."

Life works that way in my world, I wanted to say. My horses and animals meant everything to me, but as a farmer who saved all year to cover a possible poor crop yield, Chris viewed our finances from a different perspective.

"I studied our budget and came up with a total of twenty-five hundred dollars, Haley. That's the highest we can go, including the money you raised online."

The amount stuck in my throat. If I had to let Nevada go, I would die inside. Some of the horses went for eighty-five hundred dollars. I had to take matters into my own hands, to find a way to win Nevada while maintaining peace in my marriage.

I didn't sleep well, tossing and turning most of the night while thinking about the competition that started tomorrow, as well as the auction on Saturday. I had a horrifying dream the familiar man and boy won Nevada, and I cried hard when I had to say goodbye to her.

The following day the sun shone, but the chill in the air matched my dreary thoughts. A handful of people stopped by Nevada's stall to ask questions about her. I was upfront and honest with them about how I wished to keep her, and most people respected the strong bond we had developed, except for the pushy man and son combo. I heard the heavy cowboy boots plodding down the barn aisle toward us. His cologne wafted through the air, not mixing well with the sweet smell of hay. A toxic combination, in my opinion. Would he not stop until he won my horse?

I stood inside her stall, brushing her, wanting to relish every quiet moment we had left together. His presence disrupted my thoughts.

"Can I pet her?" the boy asked his father, who turned his questioning gaze on me.

I shook my head. "She doesn't tolerate strangers well and has never been around them much." I thought he'd understand my meaning, that Nevada wasn't for him or his boy, but he continued to push hard.

"The horse is here competing, so she must be fine."

I stopped brushing and stared at him, wishing for him to disappear and leave me alone. I took in his long hair, his chest and bicep muscles bulging from beneath his too-tight sweatshirt, his flared jeans, and the monstrous-sized boots that created the plodding noises in the aisle.

"Tell me more about her." His oversized hand made the pen look tiny as he held it between his huge fingers, ready to write in a little blue notebook.

I thought I had said enough but apparently not. "She doesn't like strangers. She's been a challenge to train and has bonded only to me, not even to my husband. I'd like to keep her."

He paused, pen stilled, and stared at me with intense eyes. His intimidation technique didn't work on me. Goodbye to my pleaser tendencies.

"She's at the competition, so I don't understand. I thought every horse in the adult competition, the youth excluded, were up for adoption. Am I misunderstanding?"

I fought a groan. "No, you are correct, but I plan to bid on her." I wanted to explain how most people respected the trainer's desire to hold on to their horse but didn't waste my breath. I refused to argue with him.

Breathe in, breathe out slower.

"I was told to come here because all horses were up for bid, that they go for good prices." He shook his head in frustration. "But everyone I talk to wants to keep their horse. It makes no sense."

Frustration mounted inside me like a bronco plotting to ditch its unwanted rider.

"Training a mustang from wild to mild is an unbelievable bonding experience," I explained with feigned patience. "It's a challenging but rewarding three months, and that's why trainers want to return home with their horses." My reasoning fell flat on the ground between us.

"She's my first choice," he said, nodding at Nevada, not acknowledging what I had said to him. "She's one of the biggest horses here and beautiful enough to attract a lot of attention. My customers like pretty."

And they wanted an animal that enjoyed being pet by strangers. Nevada wasn't that horse.

"You'll be seeing more of us," he promised as he flashed another admiring glance over Nevada before leaving with his son.

I pressed my fingers into the bridge of my nose to regain my focus. I refused to let this man waltz in here and threaten to destroy what I had worked so hard to accomplish for the past one hundred days. The competition was stressful enough, and tension coursed through my veins like acid, burning me from the inside out.

I sensed the auction would test me to the fullest. If I had known I would face this level of intense turmoil once we made it to Kentucky, I wouldn't have entered the program.

Who was I kidding? The makeover was the opportunity of my life.

I reminded myself to keep my emotions in check. If keeping Nevada was meant for me, then my dream wouldn't pass me by.

I had almost regained control of my emotions until a couple approached the stall.

"Isn't she gorgeous," the woman exclaimed, nudging her husband as she peeked into Nevada's stall. She then turned toward me. "I'm Heidi and this is Dennis. Can you tell us about her?"

I inhaled a calming breath before I answered. "She's been a challenge to train, but I fell in love and want to buy her." I didn't want to mislead anyone.

"I respect that, but please tell me more about her," Heidi said as she pulled a pen and notebook out of her purse. I found her relentless too. I wasn't cut out for this.

"She's bold and has stranger danger. She hasn't let anyone handle her except me." I wanted to remain positive but honest. "Her first reaction is aggression, but once she understands and agrees with what you're asking, she won't have an issue with the task again."

Heidi nodded and scribbled words on paper. My internal

radar went off, and I listed her in the category as a real threat along with the man and son. If only people empathized that I wanted to keep the horse I worked so hard to train.

When they left, Chris approached the stall. "More interested people?"

"Unfortunately." I sidled up to him. "Oh, Chris. What am I going to do? I can't stand the thought of losing Nevada." My heart practically ripped out of my chest.

"Have faith, Haley. It's not in your hands." He pulled me into his arms and gave me a long hug. "Whatever is meant to happen will, and you have to trust it will work out the right way."

"That's easier said than done."

"Of course. That's why it's called faith."

Katie and Lisa stopped by our stall for a visit.

"How's Nevada handling all the activity here?" Katie asked.

"She's doing well, calm even. I think she's tired from the long trip." I rubbed my hand across Nevada's soft neck, truly appreciating every moment with her. Love took on a new meaning. "Have you had a lot of bidder interest?"

"Too much for comfort," Katie said, rubbing her face as if trying to wash away the stress.

I wasn't the only one feeling the increasing tension the closer we approached the dreaded event. "It's too much on top of all we've been through," I said, wanting to empathize with her.

"Agreed." Katie leaned against the stall, her face tense, and she looked tired. "I haven't had a lot of interest, maybe because Bonnie is smaller, but there's been enough to put me on edge."

Lucky her, although any amount of bidder interest was too much. No one deserved to have their horse swept away, but then again, we knew the stakes upfront when we signed up for the program.

Nevada didn't need to experience the stress of having to trust new people. Unpleasant memories popped into my mind as I remembered all too well the lasso incident, being dumped on the ground, and Nevada kicking Lisa. I didn't wish those experiences upon anyone, but I also wouldn't trade our journey for anything. I was getting a crash course on life.

"How about you?" Katie asked. "Anyone interested in Nevada?"

I sighed, trying to remain positive but to no avail. "Too interested. They love her size, particularly one man and his son. They have visited Nevada's stall three times already to ask questions and wanting to pet her, although I warn them each time. They are relentless."

Lisa frowned. "Not good. Do you think they will bid on her?"

"I'm almost certain of it." I fought back tears burning my eyelids. "They want her as a carriage horse in downtown Charleston. Can you imagine? Nevada is good at a lot of things, but she isn't cut out for that."

Katie scoffed. "For starters, Nevada doesn't like people." She grimaced, likely thinking about Lisa's bruise. "It wouldn't be good if some unsuspecting kid reached out to pet her."

The thought made me shudder. "Nope. I need to make them understand that Nevada isn't the best horse for the job. But how?"

"Flat out tell them," Lisa suggested.

"I pretty much did, but maybe I need to be more straightforward." I stepped from the stall. Nevada tried to follow me, but I slid the door closed between us.

"Don't be so polite," Lisa said, standing still as Nevada approached the bars of the stall window to sniff her. It was the closest she had purposely ventured to someone else.

"That's progress," Katie said, not moving to avoid spooking Nevada. "But she has a long way to go."

"Amazing," I said, surprised by Nevada's interest in Lisa. "Maybe she's becoming more confident."

Nevada touched Lisa's hand through the bars for a fraction of a second before she jumped and ran to the corner of the stall. Lisa glanced at the time. "Let's get down to the ring early to let our horses acclimatize to the activity and loudspeaker."

"Great idea." My nerves twitched. The show was about to

begin. "I'll meet you at the arena in twenty minutes."

I hurried into the tack stall to change into dress jeans, cowboy boots, a nice shirt, and pulled on the trusty hat that Chris bought me. Time to *cowgirl up*.

Chris approached the stall. "Remember one thing," he said with a proud, lopsided grin on his face. "You signed up for the makeover because you wanted to save a wild horse, to give her a chance for adoption and a happy life. No matter what happens, your intentions are from the heart, so you are both winners."

My soul practically melted into a puddle at my feet. He was right. "Thank you, sweetheart. I love you." I slipped into his arms and kissed him.

He squeezed me into a tight hug. "Go get 'em, tiger."

My mom joined us. "You've got this. You'll do fine."

I appreciated their support and trust in me. They were right. I needed to believe in myself and my horse. Today required a demonstration of my skill set to catch Nevada in a round pen, a mock-grooming task, and stepping into the unfamiliar trailer after the long ride to Kentucky. She had improved on trailering, but not enough to...

Stop doing that. Here I was, putting up mental roadblocks of failure in my way.

Stop, just stop.

Chris led the way to the crowded warm-up arena. Day one of the competition meant no turning back, no more innocent days at home bonding with my mare. If we competed well, the increased bidders were certain to circle like vultures. If we failed to win the makeover, there would be no prize money, and I could pretty much kiss my sweet mare goodbye.

THE STRESSFUL TESTS

I waited in the warm-up ring with Nevada while standing near Lisa and Katie. We remained silent, each one of us dealing with our own complex set of emotions.

The grooming task didn't concern me as much as the daunting trailer, and I predicted that task would be our nemesis.

As we waited our turn, I grew thirsty, sick to my stomach, and my nerves were edgy.

Chris flashed me a thumbs-up, keeping a wide berth from Nevada. "Remember, you achieved your goal of making it here. The rest is a reward."

I looked back at him and forced a smile to show my gratitude.

The staff announced I was on deck. Chris blew me a kiss, and my mom wished me good luck, along with Katie and Lisa.

Let's do this, Nevada. My words remained obstructed in my throat, but I knew she understood my silent thoughts. I felt an encouraging pat on my back from some brave soul, probably Chris, and then I led Nevada forward toward the gate of the arena. A man closed it behind us after we entered.

Nevada balked for a moment as the bright overhead lights shined into our eyes. The stands held groups of people but nothing like what the auction would hold tomorrow. We had been in the expansive indoor arena with other horses, but this was our first time alone.

Pull it together, ground yourself. I inhaled my signature long breath, and Nevada picked up on my subtle shift in focus and calmed down.

We strode toward the round pen as the announcer talked in his deep, rich accent. "Hip number two in the arena for you now. Nevada is a five-year-old mare from Triple B Nevada herd management area, trained and handled by Haley Wilson from Scotland Neck, North Carolina. She lives there with her husband, Chris."

They will only know we are nervous if we tell them. Shake it off!

I tuned into Nevada as we approached the gate of the round pen, barely hearing the announcer talk about my history, my horsemanship beginning at a very young age, and being asked to train horses at fourteen.

His voice blurred, and I led Nevada to the opposite end of the pen to remove the halter to demonstrate how easy she was to catch, but she misunderstood and thought I gave her the cue to lie down. With a calm demeanor, I distracted her from rolling in the dirt by walking away, except she followed me to the gate, as if confused why I left her behind. She grew bored with me when I closed the latch, then she walked away to sniff the ground, pawing, and even circling to find that perfect spot to roll in the deep arena dirt. I hurried back inside, rushing to catch her. Thankfully, she stood still and I slid the halter on her with ease.

Pleased with how our first obstacle went, I led her out of the round pen to an upturned barrel with a brush on top. Sitting to the right of us in the arena, not more than twenty feet away, four people judged our every move. I swallowed hard and ran the brush over both sides of Nevada while holding on to the lead rope. I had seen others drop the rope to the ground, having taught the horse to stand still without contact, but I didn't chance it. I envisioned her taking off without me in the vast ring.

When I placed the brush back on the barrel, Nevada stepped forward a couple of steps, perhaps anticipating our next move. I asked her to trot the short distance to a cone, something she usually excelled at, but she lagged at the walk. My encouragement failed, so I swung the lead rope at her and clucked my tongue, but she stared at the looming trailer ahead. It perched in our path like a giant monster, basked in the purple hue of the overhead light that glared in our eyes. That must be why she didn't trot for me. We stopped at the cone, backed up several steps, then I picked up each of her hooves while the judges watched. Proud, I resisted the urge to pat her while in the competition and attempted to trot toward the trailer with confidence. She balked several times over.

Come on, she knows how to do every task required.

In our trainers' meeting this morning, the familiar halter man, as I liked to call the staff member, mentioned that if a horse refused to load in a new trailer, it was the trainer's fault. Horses picked up on our intentions and worries.

Enough. We can do this.

I visualized Nevada walking straight into the trailer, but she had different intentions. She flat out refused by planting her feet in the dirt. I believed she had made up her mind before the cone. Whatever the case, she had no plans to load, and if she didn't, it was likely we lost our chance at the prize money.

I presented the trailer to her again, but no chance. One thing about Nevada was she held strong to her own opinions and wasn't about to perform any task unless I had her buy-in. I didn't know if we were disqualified, as in eliminated for only this class, which still meant we could compete in the other classes. She'd have to face the auction no matter what level of success we experienced. The trailer was the last obstacle and the announcer excused us from the ring.

A man opened the gate for us to leave. My family greeted me in the wide chute that led to the warm-up ring, having watched my performance from the railing. I was so glad they were there to support me. A wave of emotion rushed through me.

The handling and conditioning class was over. *Thankfully*!

I tried to let go of the sense of failure at not trotting or completing the trailer task.

"Way to go." Katie gave me a thumbs-up as we passed by her. "Don't worry about the trailer."

I pushed my thoughts aside. "Thanks, and best of luck! Knock off their socks." She nodded at me and had to straighten her cowboy hat before she walked Bonnie toward the arena gate. I held back near the fence to watch her compete.

I tried to observe but didn't have the best view. I saw enough to know they had a slight bobble or two, but Bonnie loaded into the trailer with ease. I heard the crowd cheer and knew the risk of interested observers was real.

When Katie walked out the gate, I gave her a high five for a job well done and then hurried to the barn to tuck Nevada inside her stall so we could return to the stands to watch Lisa compete. My family followed at a safe distance, offering me praise and encouragement for the upcoming riding test. Their support gave me a sense of appreciation for being here in Kentucky against all odds. What a sense of awe.

Stomp, stomp, stomp. I caught a whiff of strong cologne. My brain practically froze like the brain freeze that came from eating a cherry snow cone too fast. The man with the heavy footsteps and his son showed up as I stepped out to close the stall door. *Not now.* I didn't want to make time for him and wanted to return to my friends.

I started to walk away when he said, "She looks trained to me, except for the trailer incident."

I didn't plan to get into a training discussion with him, now or ever. I had to fight my people-pleasing urge to talk to him and made myself continue to walk.

"Thank you," I said, calling behind me. I mentally patted myself on the back at the progress I made so far, but that didn't stop thoughts from popping into my head. I hoped the man and his boy had sense enough not to stick their hands in Nevada's stall. Chris and my mom, walking Stubby on a leash, joined me on my quest to return to the arena.

"When is that guy going to let up?" Mom asked, sighing.

"I hope soon." I rolled my eyes. "He pops up around every corner."

Chris remained quiet, and I suspected he might feel guilty about the cap on my bidding ability. If that man won my horse, I would puke for a week.

We showed up in time to see Lisa and Magnolia enter the arena. I led the way through the numerous horses at the gate, made our way up five rows of bleachers, and chose an unoccupied row of seats. Lisa and Magnolia seemed calm in the arena, as if they had competed a hundred times over. We watched them enter the round pen, where she let Magnolia loose and left her behind to demonstrate how easy she was to catch. Magnolia stared at Lisa, confused until she reentered, and they reconnected with ease. She brushed her horse with the lead rope dangling to the ground, an advanced movement. Their smooth navigation of each object made the tasks look easy, but I knew firsthand they were not.

When they finished, the audience applauded, and someone whistled. From the reaction of the crowd, several people seemed interested in Magnolia.

We returned to the barn to check on Nevada before taking time out of the day to mentally prepare for the class this afternoon called Mustang Maneuvers.

I stopped short. Chris rammed into the back of me, and I had to steady myself. "Sorry, sweetheart," he said from behind me.

I was unable to answer as I stared at the overbearing man who stood at Nevada's stall, talking to her.

Leave my horse alone, I wanted to say but didn't. No matter how much I disliked him near Nevada, he had a right to stand anywhere he wanted. I growled under my breath.

"Down, girl," Chris whispered. His comment surprised me.

I don't care. Stop being the nice girl all the time.

I strode toward the man. He backed out of my way as I opened the stall door to visit my horse.

"Just so you know, she's the only horse I'm bidding on."

I ignored him, petting Nevada's side like I had a brush in my hand.

"I one hundred percent want her. Nothing will change my mind."

Right now, I hated him, but I didn't believe in *hate*. Okay, I despised him. Was that better?

Not really.

I inhaled a long breath to better deal with him.

"Since you are ignoring me, I will see you in the arena. Be prepared to say goodbye to your mare because she will soon belong to me." He turned on the heels of his thick boots and strode off with his boy following.

I gasped at the man's nasty words. My belly ached as if he had sucker punched me in the gut.

The world blurred around me. Who would willingly sign up for such torture? Chris's words broke through my thoughts. "If someone wins her, then you saved a mustang."

But I was drowning in pain. I buried my head in Nevada's neck and let the tears flood like a torrential downpour. Wailing noises filled the stall space around me.

"You okay?" I heard Chris ask.

I shook my head. He let me be for now, but I sensed him nearby.

After I had the cry of my life, he returned to the stall.

"Come on," he said, taking my hand.

We walked Stubby to our favorite grassy hill behind the arena to allow me to recover. When we reached our little spot, Chris leaned back on his elbows, chewing on a piece of grass with his cowboy hat tipped down to shade his eyes. I sat up, watching Stubby sniff the ground.

I tried hard to dig myself out of the depressing hole I had fallen into and tried to focus on the time I shared with Chris and Stubby. The downtime was what horse shows were made of, moments where memories were born. Many childhood years I had spent with my horse friends, eating from food trucks, sitting in the stall area in hammocks, or spraying off horses together in the wash stall. Life was about friends and family, something we all needed reminders of occasionally.

I lay back next to Chris and pressed the left side of my body into him to absorb his warmth. I hadn't realized how much emotion I had put into the last hundred days and cherished every second of the short hours that remained. These precious moments might be memories I'd have to draw on if I lost Nevada forever. Somehow, I planned to keep her in my life, to reach out to the new owner and plead they let me stay in touch. I hoped, begged, and wished it wasn't that awful man.

"What are you thinking?" Chris asked.

I stared up at the white fluffy clouds in the blue sky to buy me a few seconds before answering. I didn't want him to feel guilty about the situation, but we believed in full transparency with each other. I swallowed hard, my throat burning, and I saw evidence of concern for me in his eyes.

"This is the end of the line, Chris. Everything I've worked so hard for will be decided in the next twenty-four hours."

"I know you love Nevada but remember …"

I stared at him. "That doesn't make letting go easier. And that man … I don't consider him a good home."

Chris turned away. I knew he had a difficult time handling my emotions. So did I. He was hurting just knowing I was, and he couldn't reach out to soothe me anymore than I could him.

"This is different, Chris. Think about all Nevada and I have been through. I know we've gone down this road before when I didn't want to give up one of my strays."

He glanced at me. "Haley, I knew this was going to be hard on you."

He had tried to warn me. I hadn't listened.

The pain ripped through me, shredding my heart to pieces at the thought of handing Nevada off to someone else, especially knowing she might be on the streets pulling a carriage. How was I supposed to survive this? My throat burned as if I had swallowed a hot fire poker, but I made myself speak. "I appreciate all your support through this journey. I don't want us to suffer financial difficulty over me bidding a higher amount, but I don't know how I'm going to handle losing her."

"Is there a chance of winning prize money?"

I sat up, drawing my knees to my chest and hugging them. "I don't know." Pressure filled me to perform well. The winnings would go a long way to help me bid on Nevada, and they'd be much more than what we'd allocated for my bid. "I feel like a failure, like I've already lost her."

"Keep fighting, Haley."

Stubby hopped up and licked me on my cheek. I wrapped him in my arms and held onto him.

The Mustang Maneuvers class was here before I knew what happened. My family stood by me in the warm-up ring as I sat on Nevada and waited for my turn. It was chilly this afternoon, at least twenty degrees cooler than back home, and Nevada seemed a little friskier than usual. I chose to wear a long-sleeved black shirt to help me stay warm, black jeans, cowboy boots, and a helmet for safety instead of my cowboy hat.

Someone walked up behind us and touched Nevada's butt before I was able to warn them. Thank goodness she didn't react. My worst fear next to losing her at the auction was she'd kick some unsuspecting victim. I reasoned Nevada was tired and didn't want to put the effort into responding.

Katie had already shown Bonnie before we arrived at the arena but mentioned she had done well. We were running late thanks to a wardrobe mishap, which my mom solved by finding my shirt in the backseat of the truck. Katie was up in the stands, waiting for me to perform. She was a good friend, one I had grown to trust and value, as well as Lisa. We shared laughs, frustrations, and supported one another.

The man at the gate flagged that I was on deck.

"Good luck," my mom and Chris said at the same time.

I nodded and focused on my breathing. We had come this far, from day one to day one hundred, and had faced many roadblocks and barriers blocking our path, and now it was time to shine. We still held the possibility to place in the ribbons and to win prize money.

I cued Nevada to walk forward, and we stopped at the gate as the person ahead of us performed. I shouldn't have watched because I realized how stiff the competition was. The horse and rider were smooth, working well together, every transition made to look easy. Her horse had almost completed the obstacle course before she spooked when someone in the stands stood as the horse passed by.

We hadn't practiced much with dealing with an audience, either.

It was our turn to enter. We walked in, the purple cast from the indoor light shining in our eyes. The crowd had grown since we performed this morning, and it seemed they were right on top of us with more movement and clapping than the audience at the Raleigh fairgrounds. This was the first time I had ridden Nevada in the arena alone, and she noticed the crowd too. We were both on edge.

I wondered if the man and the boy sat in the stands, watching us.

Focus. Tune everyone out. It's just Nevada and me.

The same deep voice of the announcer sounded over the loudspeaker. "Number two for you now. Nevada, a five-year-old buckskin mare from Nevada. Trained and ridden by Haley Wilson from Scotland Neck, North Carolina."

I asked her for the trot, and she gave me a nice even pace, but the crowd distracted her. About a quarter of the way along the edge of the audience, a spectator shifted in her seat, and Nevada scooted away from her. I tried to keep her steady, but Nevada kept a sharp eye focused on them in case of danger. She chewed the bit with anxiety, and because her neck bent toward the crowd, she was difficult to steer. We managed to trot to the far end of the arena, which was not nearly as packed with onlookers.

I cued her for an extended trot, not necessarily faster, but with a longer stride, and then we broke into the canter to show off her movement and control. She performed everything I asked, trying hard to please me, but we were off the mark with each maneuver, doing our best but not polished enough to place in the competitive class. We trotted and then halted, backed up several beautiful steps, and then pivoted in a half circle to reverse direction.

We had a rough time demonstrating the same sequence of moves in the opposite direction, but we pulled off the tasks. When we finished, I patted her, focusing more on rewarding her than caring what the judges thought, and the audience clapped. She startled and scooted forward but then regained composure to walk out of the arena.

My family climbed down from the stands and met me at the gate as we walked through the small handful of awaiting horses and into the warm-up arena. I lost track of Katie and Lisa.

When we returned to the barn, guess who waited in front of Nevada's stall? Yep, the annoying man and his offspring. Didn't he have a life outside of us? This was almost bully behavior. He haunted my dreams at night and my thoughts during waking hours.

"Nice performance. She's a keeper," he said, as if I needed his approval.

I didn't have the emotional strength to answer, and for once, I didn't care if I came off rude.

"What amount do you plan to bid on her?" he asked as though wanting to make sure he beat my highest amount. I found the man relentless and cruel.

My top dollar wasn't his business. More than anything, I wished he wouldn't be the person to win my sweet Nevada.

THE AUCTION

Today was the day that would change my life forever.
We arrived at the Kentucky Horse Park early in the morning to feed Nevada before an eventful day. This might be my last time feeding her breakfast. In fact, today was full of possible last moments, such as the last time cleaning her stall, brushing her, and having the pleasure to ride her.

I tried to fight back my emotions, my eyes burning, and a lump in my throat.

While I picked her stall clean, I tried to keep my black show outfit dust free. Several people stopped by to ask questions about her. They kept notebooks to keep track of the details to help them make their final choice.

"How old is she?" a lady asked.

"Five."

Another woman wanted to know Nevada's height, if she was gentle, how her training went. I answered all the questions, my mind in a haze. How was I supposed to concentrate on our last class of the morning with all these inquiries?

I just wanted to enjoy my life with Nevada. No distractions, no questions, just quiet time.

I must be a sadist to bring this pain on myself. My soul hurt. Nevada was my baby. If I lost her, it would be like losing my own kid.

"You ready?" My mom interrupted the relentless questions.

I glanced at the time. "Wow, I didn't realize it was so late." I finished cleaning the stall and then brushed Nevada, wishing I could take as long as I wanted to cherish every second. Mom brought me the saddle and pad, and I placed them on Nevada's back before tightening the girth, remembering when she scooted off to the side and left the saddle on the ground at her feet. I chuckled at the memory.

Those precarious days seemed so long ago.

If I'd learned anything, it was perseverance, and to believe, to keep believing, and to believe some more.

Chris showed up after my mom, and together we walked to the warm-up arena. Trail Obstacle was the last class unless by some miracle we made it into the championships. The idea of riding her without a bridle and saddle to music seemed a dream. I hadn't even practiced my freestyle routine because I really didn't believe we had a chance to make it to the finals. I saw several of the other competitors' outstanding rides. It amazed me at how much they'd accomplished in such a short time. But if I didn't compete in the championships, there would be no prize money, which meant no extra money for the auction.

Do the best we can.

"Go get'em!" Chris said, grinning at me.

"You've got this, sweetheart." My mom reached over and squeezed my thigh as I sat on my horse.

My nerves twitched. A man opened the gate for us, and we entered. I was used to the purple hue shining in my eyes at times from the overhead lightning and suspected Nevada no longer minded, either.

The same man with the deep, calm voice introduced us. We walked past the first cone and headed toward two poles placed on the ground. Nevada lowered her head to study them, hesitating briefly, but then walked over them with ease. I wanted to tell her she was a good girl, but the judges watched our every move. I asked her for the trot, and to my delight, she picked it up like a pro. We executed a serpentine, an S-shaped pattern, through three cones. Nevada again surprised me with her willingness to please me. Our steering remained somewhat off the mark, requiring a little extra effort on my part.

I felt something in my back pocket trying to slip out. My phone! I was so nervous before the class, I forgot to remove my big orange cell phone and hand it to Chris. I hoped she didn't spook if it fell out and tried to focus on the trail obstacles and maneuvers before me.

We cantered a large figure-eight, bobbling at the trot where the two circles crossed. We picked up a canter once more and headed toward a three-sided box made from poles. I didn't care at this point if we won or not, Nevada made me proud. As we grew closer, she hesitated, broke to a trot instead, and we had a little scuffle where I had to convince her that we were, in fact, going to trot into that boxed-off area and then perform a sliding stop. Instead, she broke to a walk, so no sliding stop, but I was pleased. I loved this horse and knew she tried her best. Nerves had a way of getting to both of us.

I aimed her at the pole, and she stepped over with ease. No worries. The bridge told a different story. She surprised me, as it was something she had done at least twenty times before, but she balked.

Come on, Nevada. You've done this obstacle in the warm-up arena without fault.

Perhaps the purple hue played tricks with her mind. I encouraged Nevada forward, but she walked sideways a few steps, all the while keeping her gaze fixed on the bridge. I presented it to her again, but she walked sideways along it, stopping once to sniff the wood. At home, if Nevada worried about a task, I took my time and utilized training tools and patience to help her grow comfortable with scary obstacles, but here, she either crossed the bridge or she didn't. We were already out of the ribbons and prize money, so her training came first. I let her take her time making peace with the bridge.

The calm man's voice sounded over the loudspeaker. "Go

ahead and move to the next obstacle, please."

It's okay, Nevada. Don't worry about it.

She relaxed as if she read my mind.

We stepped sideways along a single pole, and then trotted to a makeshift gate, where I had to reach down and open it for her to move through, and then close it behind us. The crowd applauded, making me even prouder of my horse, and we left the arena.

Even though I knew we didn't place, I smiled and patted her neck. "Good girl, Nevada. You did a great job."

My mom and Chris reached us, my mom placing her hand on my thigh for support, making sure to stay outside Nevada's kick zone. "Way to go, girls."

Chris smiled at me and winked.

Katie grinned from the bleachers and gave me a thumbs-up.

We might not have placed, but we were at the makeover, and we finished another class. A long month ago I didn't think we'd achieve this level.

After we brought Nevada to the stall, Chris and I took Stubby for a walk to our grassy hill to grab a moment of quiet before the big auction. This quiet spot was perfect to ease my nerves. We lay back on the lawn, Chris with a piece of grass poking from his mouth, me bracing myself on my elbows. Stubby smelled the ground.

I wanted him to ask me how I was handling all of this, but he didn't. Looking at his tense jaw, I realized how stressed he was too.

The sky was cloudy today, and the temperature a bit cooler. At home, I'd be wearing cutoff shorts, a tank top, and wishing for a swim in the river.

I spoke without taking my eyes off the gray sky. It looked as though rain were about to dump on us.

"When I first started this challenge," I explained, "I wanted to prove myself to my family, to my clients, even to myself that I had what it took for people to pay me as a trainer. I wanted to quit my job to train horses. But I learned an important lesson." My voice quivered, and I wanted Chris to hug me, to hold me, to tell me Nevada was mine no matter what, but I knew he dealt with his own complicated emotions.

The expression in his eyes softened. "What lesson was that?"

I swallowed hard. "My own ego was at play. Hitting the ground hard a couple of times changed me." I paused to swallow hard. *Go on, confess.* "I was so full of myself and my ability when I signed up for this program. I thought, no worries. I've trained undomesticated horses before, so no problem. I had wanted to ride her without a bridle or saddle in front of all these people at the championships, but we won't qualify."

We hadn't been in the ribbons, but Katie received one ribbon and Lisa qualified for freestyle championships, placing high in every class.

"Does that bother you?" he asked, his lips moving around the blade of grass in his mouth.

I shrugged. "Not really, other than not having the prize money to up the ante for the auction."

He grimaced.

"I'm not trying to make you feel bad," I said. I would be lying if I didn't admit, at least to myself, that the two-thousand-dollar limit concerned me. Don't get me wrong, I was grateful I had that much to bid, but from the amount of people asking questions about Nevada, the risk of losing her gnawed at my mind.

I had to figure out a way to fix this awful mess.

The time flew by too fast. My mom found us on the hill and said, "You need to get ready for the auction."

No! I wanted to yell, to scream, to refuse. Nobody would listen to my outburst anyway.

My throat squeezed as if someone held their hand on it, trying to choke the life out of me. My eyes grew moist, and I sniffled.

Chris took hold of my hand. The three of us walked Stubby back to the barn in silence.

I changed into one of my show outfits and enjoyed long, quiet silence in the stall with Nevada. My family respected our time together and had left us alone.

"Nevada, this might be our last sprinkle of time left together. Just know you will always be my heart horse." She nuzzled me. I fought off tears and rubbed her soft nose. "No matter who wins you, know I will find you and keep in touch. You will be fine."

She nudged me, and a giggle slipped from my sad self.

I slipped her a carrot and enjoyed the sound of her munching. It's the little things in life that bring a person joy.

"Haley, it's time," my mom said in a low voice from outside the stall.

"Okay." I put the saddle on Nevada and then the bridle, possibly one last time. Everything held that level of importance. I would hang the bridle up in the tack room with her name marked above it, never to be used on another horse again.

I led her out of the stall, and Chris and my mom followed us to the crowded warm-up arena. After mounting Nevada, I walked her around to ward off the nervous edge that followed us like a dirt cloud on a dusty morning. I stopped next to Lisa and Katie.

"Congratulations on making it to the championship round," I said to Lisa. "You and Magnolia deserve accolades. What an accomplishment."

Lisa grinned from ear to ear. "Thank you, but we all deserve a big pat on the back. The makeover was an amazing journey. And I learned something from it."

"What's that?" Katie asked, relaxed in the saddle as if she were exhausted. We all were. It had been a long voyage, and we were about to dock the ship. The auction was here at last.

"I learned that I want to keep Magnolia." Lisa patted her horse. "She gave me everything she had, worked hard, and taught me a lot."

My heavy heart surged with excitement for her.

"You have a lot of bidders wanting her," I said, not to discourage her but to prepare her for the high bids.

"I know. It will be rough, but if I win the championship, I will use every penny to win her back."

At least she had that option. Katie and I were at the mercy of a miracle.

Thump, thump, thump. My jaw tightened.

The man and his boy approached me. "Good luck out there." He grinned and I fought of nausea. "Can we pet her?"

I shook my head to warn him. "She doesn't like strangers, and she's exhausted from the long trip and competing. She's rather cranky." *Like me*, I wanted to add. My behavior didn't reflect my usual sunny self, *but dang it*, this was more difficult than I ever imagined.

He ignored my advice and reached out to pet her neck. Nevada pinned her ears. She bared her teeth and reached out to snap at him. He pulled his hand away and stepped back just in time to avoid getting bitten.

I sat on her back, stunned, but had a flashback to that first day in the round pen when she charged me with bared teeth.

The man pushed his son behind him, and then they left without comment.

Lisa gasped. "Wow! Reminds me of the day she kicked me."

"Some people don't listen," Katie said.

I closed my eyes, drew in a long breath.

Chris approached us. "I saw what happened."

I sucked in a slow breath, exhaled slower to regain my composure.

The man at the gate called us in as a group. My heart slammed against my chest, and my breathing became fast.

"Haley, have faith," Chris said in his calm voice. "Believe in miracles."

My eyes burned, and a tear trickled down my cheek. Chris touched my hand. "You've got this."

My mom approached us. "Haley, love you." She held up her hand and crossed her fingers.

Katie turned her horse toward the gate and walked off.

"Go get 'em, sweetheart," Chris said, his face tight with concern.

"Thanks for your support." I tried hard to keep my emotions under control.

I walked into the arena, almost loving every last second of the purple hue glaring in my eyes. I steered Nevada to the corner of the arena to hang out with Katie, my heavy heart dragging in the arena dirt behind me.

I focused on swallowing. Watching one horse after another get auctioned off to a hungry crowd scared me beyond anything I had experienced. I tried so hard to train Nevada, to love and believe in her, to do my very best. The makeover seemed surreal. All this time I had wanted nothing more than to prove to everyone else what a great trainer I was.

For real? Who really cared? The thought seemed ridiculous now that I sat here in the arena, watching the horses being auctioned off. What a cruel joke! I couldn't take this, not another minute. I wanted to gallop out of the ring and never look back.

But that was a coward's way. I had entered this contest because I wanted Nevada to have a good home.

She does have a good home!

My home! Our home!

I'd find a way to support Nevada by training horses and teaching lessons.

I stared up at the bright lights. *Please, oh please, let Nevada come home with me. I was misguided. I was a pleaser, but I no longer care what people think of me. If they want to hire me as a trainer, fine. If they don't, no worries.*

Nevada was the real prize, not the approval of people. It was always about Nevada. I wanted her to have the best life possible. *If it isn't me, then let her find a great home.*

Tears ran down my cheeks. I turned my face away from my friend, afraid Katie would see me cry, but then I turned back. I no longer cared what people thought. *Cry, Haley, if you want to cry.*

It seemed the makeover journey was a mixed bag of emotions. I mean, who in the world wanted to go through losing their best friend, having their heart ripped from their chest?

Nothing had been easy from the get-go. I had to fight for every short-lived accomplishment, and this was my reward, an auction to take away my dream of bringing my mare back home with me.

"Hip number two," the halter man called, but the world was a blur for me.

"Haley, that's you," Katie said frowning. I saw tears smudged on her cheeks.

I looked up and resisted the urge to wipe my face clean from my own tears. "Let's go, Nevada."

We walked to where the auctioneer, the halter man, and the announcer stood. I passed by them, circling as if I were calm. Chris said to have faith that the right person would win.

"Nevada," the halter man said. "A five-year-old buckskin mare. Gathered from the Triple B, Nevada herd management area. She's a big ole stout mare right here. She's going to do it all for you."

"I tell you," the halter man said, "she's got some good size on her. She's got some great color to her. They have some really cool colors out in that area and some really good horses. Good size."

"Here we go." The announcer glanced over at me, but I remained calm on the outside, although shaking on the inside.

My heart sank like a weighted fishing line in the river back home. I wanted my bed, my warm comforter, my pillow. Chris.

Believe, keep believing, and believe some more. Surrender to whatever is meant to be.

I cued Nevada to walk a large circle around the announcer without acknowledging him. I tried not to look out at the crowd. Panic rose in me, and even though I put on a casual face, I was about to vomit.

Please, oh please, let Nevada find a good home.

The auctioneer began to rattle off a string of words I didn't pretend to understand.

I couldn't continue. There was no way I wanted to lose my horse, the equine love of my life. I debated bidding more than what Chris and I agreed on.

My head spun.

My heart pounded.

I tried to keep up with the amount the auctioneer said. "Give me a thousand dollars. I've got two, three, four hundred. Six, six, give me six."

I raised my card, not able to keep up with the fast pace.

"Seven, eight, nine, a thousand," the auctioneer prattled. "Twelve, twelve. Thirteen, fourteen, sixteen."

A woman in the crowd continued to drive the bid higher. Where did she come from? She never approached me before.

"Sixteen, eighteen, nineteen. Give me nineteen."

I stopped walking in circles, my back to the crowd so I didn't see the relentless woman. What happened to the man and his son? Maybe Nevada scared him off. Nevada stood still for me, so gentle, staring at the staff members in front of me, clueless that someone was deciding her fate.

I wanted to bid higher until I won her. How would Chris handle that decision? It was too big a risk to take. He trusted me, and I knew the stakes before I entered the makeover. I had agreed not to fall in love with my mustang. I knew we didn't have more money to bid on her.

"Give me nineteen ... nineteen." He pointed at the audience. "Twenty-one hundred."

I kept my card raised high, so no one could mistake that I wanted her. Usually, people backed off when they knew the trainer, the person who worked through blood and sweat to train their mustang, wanted to own them forever. Who was this woman?

"Give me two, twenty-two hundred. Twenty-two hundred down here on the floor." I swear he pointed to the halter man, but I wasn't sure.

We were getting too close to my limit.

"Twenty-four, going to the bank, four." He rambled some fast words. "Twenty-four hundred, twenty-three, four? Sold. Twenty-three hundred, going home with Haley."

Wait! That was me!

The crowd cheered and applauded. Nevada spooked, jumped forward while I patted her neck. She whirled in a circle. I smiled big with tears dripping from my eyes. I patted her again.

Unbelievable. She was my horse. *My* horse!

The man and his son never bid on her. I rubbed Nevada's sleek neck and whispered, "You took care of the man issue on your own. Good girl." I swear she nodded her head in agreement.

Katie and I had both won our horses back. We were happy beyond belief, but there was more excitement to come. Lisa had earned her way to the championship class with Magnolia. This year's makeover was different than the past. The top-ten contestants had to wait for their own auction to find out if they were able to keep their horses.

SHOWTIME

I sat in the stands, eager, excited, and on the edge of my seat—and honestly, a wee bit sad that Nevada and I hadn't made it to the championships. But at least she was mine! With Chris and my mom positioned on one side of me and Katie on the other, we were here to watch Lisa compete in the freestyle class.

I had dreamed of competing at this level, holding onto my memory of riding Wild Man without reins, but I hadn't stopped there. I had visualized entering the final phase of the makeover without a saddle or bridle, sitting on Nevada bareback, performing maneuvers to synchronized music that only existed from clear communication and ultimate trust. The dream still lived inside of me.

Even though I missed out on participating in the championship class, I won the best prize possible. Nevada belonged to me. That was all I cared about. I glanced up and thought, miracles do happen.

The crowd packed in the stands for a full house.

The championship class started with a surge of excitement. Patriotic music shook me out of my thoughts as the horns reverberated over the loudspeaker. The familiar, comforting voice of the same announcer filled the indoor arena. "We're saving the best for last. But first, say a prayer for these skilled trainers who are doing their jobs."

The crowd stood out of respect. The announcer continued

with inspiring words about having faith and freedom, and for the leaders of our country and other countries. He allowed moments where the music played, and then he wished safe travels after the event for everyone tonight.

His voice was steady, one I'd come to rely on during the makeover.

"The mustangs are part of this country's history, prized by the earliest settlers. Few are blessed to adopt one of these living legends." Tears of emotion stirred from deep inside me as I listened to him talk.

Four riders and their horses from the Kentucky Horse Park's mounted police entered the arena to more patriotic music while carrying the flag of the United States of America. The announcer spoke with pride about our country and the brave soldiers who sacrificed themselves for our freedom. A trumpet played in the background with occasional percussion. The noble horses trotted together around the arena. When they lined up in the middle, a woman's elegant voice filled the stadium as she sang the national anthem. When she finished, the crowd clapped, and I wiped away tears from my eyes.

"Tonight, we have the privilege to watch the top ten finalists of the Mustang Makeover compete with this unique breed, the American Mustang." The announcer called out the name of each trainer, who jogged a short distance at the end of the ring to face the crowd. We cheered, yelled, and clapped when they announced Lisa Whitley.

The first class began with each contestant having ninety seconds to complete a pattern between two cones. They were judged on the horse's relaxation and confidence. Lisa and Magnolia ran through several maneuvers, including loping, sliding stops, pivoting on a tight circle, and backing up. The crowd roared, and we whooped and hollered.

The final class was the intriguing freestyle to synchronized music. *Make me proud, Lisa. I'm living through you.*

Each contestant had their own crew to bring out props and set them up when it was their turn to compete, also having chosen music to fit their performance.

"Approximately one hundred days to train these legends for Lexington, Kentucky," the announcer said, and my excitement took over.

We watched as one trainer herded a cow with his horse.

When he finished, the announcer said, "What an opportunity to observe these talented trainers who accomplished so much with their mustangs." They demonstrated amazing skills, such as galloping around to enjoyable music while dressed in costumes, walking through obstacles such as a pretend car wash made of pool noodles that touched their horse's sides. One man asked his horse to climb a ramp onto a long flatbed truck, pivoting in a tight turn to sit on a couch. A couch! The crowd roared with approval.

The old me would feel inferior, sad even, that I had accomplished no such flattering feat, but the new me wanted to learn. How they had accomplished such amazing achievements in close to a hundred days stunned me.

My mom nudged me when Lisa and Magnolia stood near the gate. "There she is."

Swallowing became difficult again with that familiar lump in my throat.

The announcer's voice sounded over the loudspeaker. "Number thirty-two up for you, next horse is named Magnolia, trainer Lisa Whitley from North Carolina." The crew set up the ring and then jogged out. The announcer called out Lisa and Magnolia's name again as they entered the arena on foot. We hollered and clapped.

Goosebumps ran through my body. Wow, Lisa made it into the finals.

Music began to play overhead, *Sweet Caroline* by Neil Diamond. Magnolia wore a large tarp draped over her body, covering everything except her head. A scary endeavor for most horses, Lisa and Magnolia made the task look easy as they remained cool, calm, and rational. Lisa slipped the tarp off her horse's rump, then mounted from the right side instead of the usual left. The crowd clapped and cheered as Magnolia stood unfazed.

They trotted off, then loped in a large circle before demonstrating a simple lead change to continue in the opposite direction as I had seen her do the day we rode at the college. The crowd clapped. The music played to perfect timing on Lisa's part and made her ride playful. They jogged to a wooden board that served as a bridge, stood on it without issue, then approached a pole on the ground. Instead of walking over it, they sidestepped the length. Another round of applause.

Magnolia trotted to an upright jump standard, retrieved a rope hanging from it, which was attached to a short wooden pole, and cantered around the arena while dragging the pole behind them. The crowd applauded, and I remembered our Christmas tree adventure the day we rode together. Dragging the tree behind us at a walk was hard enough, but to canter—impressive.

She dropped the rope and pivoted around a large ball in fun timing to the music. As she cantered to the next one, she pivoted halfway around it, and Magnolia rolled the ball with her nose and body for at least five feet as though playing.

"Thirty seconds left." The announcer's nudge spurred Lisa to finish her freestyle.

They galloped around the arena, Lisa removing her cowgirl hat and tipping it to the crowd as they cheered. Magnolia slid to a halt, backing up while the audience clapped and a few whistled, and the announcer thanked them. They pivoted in a tight circle to leave a lasting impression and left the arena.

"Told you it was going to get exciting," the announcer said in his lighthearted voice. The crowd clapped louder, and we whistled as Lisa left the ring.

I shook my head in amazement. "Incredible ride."

Royal sounding music played overhead once again. "Thank you for attending the Mustang Makeover. The trainers you've seen tonight have done an extraordinary job training these amazing mustangs from wild to mild in approximately one hundred days.

They all deserve a medal. The competition was stiff." The crowd cheered as the trainers walked into the arena without their horses.

"The winner has earned her title tonight." The announcer paused to build tension and everyone clapped. "Congratulations goes to Lisa Whitley and Magnolia, from North Carolina."

I clapped hard, tears burning my eyes, and Chris peeled a whistle. A man in a cowboy hat passed a large poster-board check to Lisa. What an incredible opportunity to see what these trainers accomplished with mustangs who roamed the desert not all that long ago.

The auction was painful to watch. One after another, the trainers who worked so hard to bring a mustang from wild to mild, raised their cards high to win back their horses. When it was Lisa's turn, my throat burned with more unshed tears.

Lisa held her card high in the air with her right hand, and I knew her well enough to notice the fear in her facial expression. One bid after another drove up the price. She rubbed Magnolia's neck with her left hand, fingers tight around the reins. The auctioneer spoke fast, but in the end, he said with enthusiasm, "Congratulations! Magnolia goes home with Lisa Whitley from North Carolina." As it turned out, Lisa's check was for the same amount she paid for her horse at auction. What a tradeoff!

EPILOGUE
THREE YEARS LATER

I waited at the gate of the arena in Lincolnton, North Carolina. The heat bore down on Nevada and me, the flies buzzing around us. A small crowd watched.

"Introducing Haley Wilson from Scotland Neck, North Carolina, and her mustang, Nevada." The announcer's voice called out over the intercom. My focus remained on Nevada, and I barely heard people clapping.

I asked her to walk into the arena at my side. After the gate shut behind us, I removed her halter and lead rope and tossed it off to the side. We walked a circle with nothing more than a short liberty whip, so I could quietly test her listening skills, and then I asked for her to trot next to me. This was my performance I didn't achieve in Kentucky. It wasn't synchronized to music but this was even better. She was my horse, and no one could take her away from me at an auction.

With a happy bounce in Nevada's step, she followed me anywhere I asked her to go. I ran backward, she trotted with me. I paused, and then asked her to sidestep toward me, and then away from me. Then, I mimicked cantering in a circle, almost like skipping but with only one leg out in front, and Nevada stayed with me. She cantered in slow motion, controlled, synchronized to my body movements, giving me more of herself than I asked.

I kicked my leg out high and slapped the ground with it, and Nevada performed the Spanish walk with me for several steps.

Nevada offered the movement out of joy, willingness to please, not by force. I barely heard the crowd clap, and someone nearby gasped. It was a difficult movement that had taken practice, and its fancy step usually impressed onlookers.

We were doing it, living my dream, having been asked to perform for a crowd of people at a mustang TIP challenge. I wanted to encourage new trainers to never give up hope on their mustangs. If I trained Nevada, so could they.

I asked her to lie down in the arena dirt, and she obliged. What a difference between where we were at the makeover to where we were today. I climbed up on her bareback and asked her to stand. She hopped up, making me slide a bit, but she made it easy to grab a chunk of mane and to stay on.

With a confidence we both had developed, and with an unbreakable bond between us, we rode around the arena in front of the crowd without a bridle or saddle. My focus remained on her. I gave her clear instructions and she listened, trying to please me. As we trotted, a feeling of freedom flowed through me. Long ago I used to ride Wild Man with no hands, and this was the best. All I carried was a short liberty whip to steer her. Her canter I could barely describe other than to say it was as if we were floating on a cloud in slow motion. This was what flying with wings must be like.

Nevada protected me, and it seemed the reason she allowed only *me* to ride her was out of loyalty. She was a one-person horse, and I was her person.

When we finished, people clapped and cheered. I inhaled a large dose of sunshine from the ninety-eight-degree day and let it fill my soul. I leaned down to pat Nevada on the neck and wrapped my arms around her. "Good girl! We did it." We performed the freestyle I had always dreamed about.

I hopped off at the gate and slipped her halter back on.

"Way to go, Haley!" My mom met me at the gate. She held my cooing baby boy in her arms, and my heart surged with deep, motherly joy.

At the beginning of the makeover, I didn't think I wanted children. Somewhere during Nevada's training for Kentucky, I began to feel a strong sense of maternal pride, and then I experienced a different kind of love besides the romantic love I felt for Chris. By the end of the journey, and after I almost lost her at the auction, I knew I had forever changed. I grew into myself by shedding my ego when I hit the dirt that awful day after my first attempt to ride her. I developed into a confident young woman who had found her own self-worth and self-love.

I had thought I could train Nevada on my own, but I fast learned that impossible feat was ego driven. Paw Paw had taught me confidence as a child, and as an adult I had found it again, the reason for my success. Believe me, relying on faith to pull me through the makeover hadn't been easy, but it led me through impossible times. Here I was, teaching students and training horses full time, helping people to achieve their own dreams. I was not the people pleaser I was before thanks to my quest to train a horse who resisted being gentled. She was the best teacher of life skills and taught me lessons I hadn't known I needed.

Despite the hardship and occasional agony of learning tough lessons, the benefits of the makeover remained a gift of a lifetime. The experience taught me more than I ever imagined.

Horses had a way of behaving like a mirror of truth to show us who we were, revealing the best and worst version of ourselves.

I thought I had saved Nevada, but in one hundred days, she had saved me too.

Dreams really do come true. Never, ever give up and leave your desires lying next to you in the dirt, for it took embracing my deepest fears to come to a mutual agreement with the lion in the pen. I had seen a whisper of a kitten in her heart, and because I kept going, my perseverance unleashed more than I imagined possible.

In the heart of a beast, I found bravery that changed my life forever.

ACKNOWLEDGMENTS

I owe thanks to many people while I learned about the history of our wild horses out west, figured out the details of training a wild mustang, and explored the emotional nuances of this story to provide as much accuracy as possible.

Abigail Hale, I thank you the moon and back. You were patient and took time out of your busy schedule to answer my many questions about your mustang journey. Good luck with all your training endeavors and your business, Abigail Hale Horses, and thank you for sharing your emotional and amazing story with me. I knew when I first met you that this story was special.

Thank you, Carley Wheelis, for sharing your story and training methods with me early on, and for introducing me to the world of wild mustangs. I owe you a mountain of appreciation for allowing me to spend days with you and Thea, watching and learning, and for sharing the Kentucky experience. I am forever grateful.

Thank you to Jessica Nelson, my amazing editor over the past couple of years. I can't imagine publishing a book without your patience, help, and positive suggestions. They say an author reflects their editor, so I hope I make you proud. You always challenge me in ways that make me a better writer. Thank you!

And last but definitely not least, a heartfelt thanks to Thomas J. Bellezza. You have opened up a new world for me and have taught me things I never imagined. You are wise far beyond your years, and I appreciate all your help! Thank you, soul warrior!

ABOUT THE AUTHOR

Lori Hayes lives in North Carolina with her family, horse, and two overly affectionate cats. Having ridden horses since the third grade on the hunter jumper circuit and showing dressage, she now owns her own once wild horse named Triton. His name fits him well because he was the king of the sea on a small, uninhabited island off the coast of the Outer Banks. Family, photography, writing, the beach, and horses are Lori's passions. She is an active member of WFWA, RWA, and HCRW. Please visit her Website at LoriHayesAuthor.com and sign up for her newsletter to stay informed about upcoming book releases, retreats, and giveaways.

Lori always loves email and getting to know you better.
Email: LoriHayesBooks@gmail.com

Please leave a review on the site you purchased Saving Nevada, good**reads**, and BookBub
Thank you!!!
~~Lori Hayes~~

Join Lori on social media:
Facebook: Facebook.com/LoriHayesAuthor
Instagram: LoriHayesAuthor
X: @LoriHayesAuthor
TikTok: @LoriHayesAuthor
YouTube: @LoriHayesMotivation

Made in the USA
Middletown, DE
16 November 2023